The Wister Trace

The Wister Trace

Classic Novels of The American Frontier

Loren D. Estleman

Jameson Books • Ottawa, Illinois

Jameson Books are available at special discounts for bulk purchases for sales promotions, premiums, fund-raising, or educational use.

Jameson Books
722 Columbus St.
Ottawa, IL 61350

(815) 434-7905

Printed in the United States of America

Distributed by Kampmann and Company, New York City.

10 9 8 7 6 5 4 3 2 1

Library of Congress Cataloging-in-Publication Data

Estleman, Loren D.
  The Wister trace.

  Bibliography: p. 129
  1. Western stories—History and criticism.
2. American fiction—20th century—History and
criticism. 3. West (U.S.) in literature. 4. Frontier
and pioneer life in literature. 5. Wister, Owen,
1860-1938—Influence. I. Title.
PS374.W4E88 1987   813'.0874'09   85-24159
ISBN 0-915463-32-6

To Dale Walker, who said:
"Would you consider expanding it?"

". . . he will never come again. He rides in his historic yesterday. You will no more see him gallop out of the unchanging silence than you will see Columbus on the unchanging sea come sailing from Palos with his caravels."

—Owen Wister, in his introduction to *The Virginian*

Contents

Preface

Santa Fe, New Mexico
July 1, 1982

The night was dry and warm, the way they all are in Santa Fe in summer. The place was Gordon D. Shirreffs' bungalow at La Posada, where a number of western writers, their spouses, and aficionados of the West had gathered to wind down after the close of the 1982 Western Writers of America convention.

Shirreffs, a legendary western writer of thirty years' experience, was holding court along with his startling and vivacious wife Alice and their grown son Brian. They were new friends to me on the occasion of my first convention, and I was content to remain in the background, sweltering in a blue suit designed for my native Michigan climate. Instead, I was introduced to a mild smiling bespectacled fellow named Dale Walker, who presented me with an inscribed copy of one of his excellent monographs on Jack London and invited me to submit something to *The Roundup*, the official publication of the WWA, which he edited. I replied that I had long thought of doing a polemic piece on the

11

development of the classic western novel. Dale said that sounded like a fine idea, and no more was said about it.

Months passed, and I was preparing for my annual deer hunting trip to northern lower Michigan when I decided at the last minute to pack a number of the western novels I had earmarked for the project. I returned a few days later, deerless but considerably better read on the subject of western fiction, and began writing. Eventually I submitted twenty-five pages dealing with ten novels under the title "The Frontier in Fiction," which I thought an inspired choice.

Dale responded enthusiastically, inviting me to expand the article to fifty pages and include more books. Change the title, he added.

A crackling correspondence followed, I suggesting titles and asking about certain books and Dale turning down my suggestions and sending the books I couldn't find. Since *The Roundup* does not pay contributors, I considered my aggrandized library adequate reward. At that time I could not know that I would someday be acknowledged the WWA's resident scholar on American western literature, or that the piece would become the first recipient of the Stirrup Award for best *Roundup* article of 1983, an award that did not exist at the time I wrote it.

The article, which ran in three parts throughout the spring and summer of 1983, covered eighteen classics and ended with an optimistic prognosis on the future of western fiction, which I am pleased to report has been confirmed by subsequent events. It was the talk of two conventions and led to a sequel in which ten additional books of equal and in some cases superior merit received attention previously denied them.

By the time the first installment was in typesetting, Dale and I had agreed to call it "Eighty Years of Western Classics." However, just as it was going to press, I wrote him asking if, in view of the seminal influence of Owen Wister's *The*

Virginian, a more appropriate and effective title might be "The Wister Trace: The First Century of Western Classics." His reply was something on the order of, "You rascal, how dare you go and come up with the perfect title." But lest I preen too much, within a week I received another note from him vetoing my subtitle and suggesting *"A* Century of Western Classics," as the other might indicate that those eighteen represented the entire lot. I acquiesced, and the article was so dubbed.

The essays that follow are a more detailed version of those that appeared in *The Roundup* in 1983 and 1985 under the respective titles "The Wister Trace" and "The Wister Trace Retraced," with more time and space devoted to each book than are permitted by the tighter restrictions of the magazine format. I make no claim that the text is exhaustive. The opinions expressed are my own, and although in some rare cases I have been forced by weight of popular sentiment to include books that I would not otherwise consider classic, what follows is subjective and open to intelligent argument. I do not, for example, consider Max Brand's *Destry Rides Again* anything more than fourth-rate pulp, and despite its robotic inclusion on almost every "best western" list published since its appearance, I have chosen to ignore it. Eugene Manlove Rhodes's oft-revered, seldom-read *Paso Por Aqui* failed the same test, although more honorably. Conversely, fans of Ernest Haycox and Luke Short will search in vain for their favorites, not because they lack merit, but because none of their titles rises significantly above their sustained level. Feminists will object to the absence of books by women authors, but as of this writing, three alone have attained deserved prominence in a genre dominated (as was the frontier itself) by men: Willa Cather, Dorothy Johnson, and Mari Sandoz. Of that trio, only one has published a full-length novel worthy of note set in the West. However, Cather's towering *Death Comes for the Archbishop* falls so far outside the genre as it is commonly perceived that it scarcely requires illumination here. Johnson's best work is in the short form, and Sandoz's books are nonfiction. A number of women writing currently show great promise, and it is hoped that the further growth of the western will attract others of their stamp. They will not be kept out much longer. Other omissions, made out of ignorance or to satisfy the exigencies of publishing, are what later editions are for. The Wister Trace is not the last word. Readers are encouraged to venture beyond its limits.

I am of course indebted to the many fine artists whose works advanced both the frontier genre and American letters; without them, our literature might still be stalled at that adolescent opus to Puritan overstatement, *Moby Dick*. Thanks are also due my fellow western writers, too many to mention, who recommended favorite books that I might otherwise have missed, at a loss to all concerned. To Gordon D. Shirreffs belongs the credit for introducing me to the man most responsible for this book, and for teaching me more about westerns over breakfast in Santa Fe than I had learned in years of writing them. Dick Wheeler, my editor at Jameson Books, merits a medal for putting up with my idiosyncrasies and for matching my enthusiasm for this book. Everything else I owe to Dale Walker, who cared enough about my aims to ask me to extend them while conducting the greatest title fight of my career. It is to him that this and all future editions of *The Wister Trace* are gratefully dedicated.

L.D.E.
Whitmore Lake, Michigan
March, 1985

Introduction
American Genesis

I. Life

In the beginning was the Land. A land so vast that at the time of its purchase from Napoleon, Thomas Jefferson predicted it would not be settled in five hundred years.

Jefferson, not known for his foresight beyond the invention of the swivel chair and a number of quotable platitudes on freedom and democracy, would be proved wrong within a bare half-century of his death, with settlers' cabins pockmarking the plains and mountains of the so-called Great American Desert and the 20,000-year reign of the nomadic Indian tribes in rapid decline after their ultimately Pyrrhic victory over a third of Custer's Seventh Cavalry at the Little Big Horn. The official closing of the frontier was the draught of a breath away, with a war in Cuba waiting in the wings to draw the nation's attention eastward for good. Wild Bill Hickok was dead, the buffalo were gone, the continent they had roamed in black herds sutured with railroad tracks. Within twenty years the first of a horde of noisy, beetle-like contraptions of flimsy sheet metal and pneumatic rubber

15

would come ticking out of the East, bringing with them the promise of proper roads and superfluity for that indestructible western icon, the man on horseback.

From Appomattox to the century's turn, the sequence of events flickers past in quickening succession like the manic motion pictures that so dedicated a frontier figure as Buffalo Bill Cody, confidant of Kit Carson and Jim Bridger, would eventually embrace as a means of telling the same tall story he had been setting to lights and music since the early 1870s. The hand that shook those of Custer and Sitting Bull would work the crank of a Pathé camera, creating an effect similar to that of Jesse James reaching across four decades to touch fingers with John Dillinger. It is with a shock of recognition that one learns that Butch Cassidy and William S. Hart were born within three years of each other.

Before Fort Sumter, the history of the American West advanced at a much more stately pace. Centuries of monopoly by the descendants of Asian tribes who had crossed the land bridge into the New World from Siberia ended when Spanish adventurers in golden armor clanked ashore at Yucatán, inadvertently trading horse mobility to the natives for their corner on a land rich in game and gold. The British followed, establishing mutually lucrative trade relations with the Indians through the oligarchic Hudson's Bay Company, whose limits were violated by lone poachers, many of whom left their bones behind to guide the mountain hermits, who in turn escorted the first of an endless chain of wagon trains west. A war with Mexico ceded more territories to the Union, and gold fever in California and homestead land in Oregon led to migrations far beyond Jefferson's provincial scope.

Then came civil war, to rip like other wars a new century from the womb of natural progression. Far from merely creating most of the icons that would shape a new folklore in the images of Frank and Jesse James and Phil Sheridan and

George Armstrong Custer and Hickok and Cody, this up-heaval would unleash a hundred thousand young men forced to maturity through the bloody funnel of combat into a postwar frontier awash in the danger and drama of which four years of bloodshed had given them only a taste. Gone to Texas the colonels and majors and captains and lieutenants and conscripts, to apply their experience in leadership and fighting to the business of taming the rangy cattle descended from Cortez's livestock. The career soldiers meanwhile es-chewed such quiet pursuits for the challenge of subjugating the heathen Indian, while others, the like of Clay Allison and the Younger brothers, lent their new skills to daylight bank robbery and murder for hire. Still more went in search of liberty or personal redemption and died in bed or between the handles of plows without once having heard a shot fired in anger.

In the thirty-year period between 1870 and 1900, fewer violent deaths occurred in Dodge City than in any major modern American population center last year alone. Yet the legend of a violent era persists, which may in part be charged to the rapid proliferation of percussion weapons west of the Mississippi after the Colt Patent Firearms Company pi-oneered in the assembly-line production of handguns ranging in size from the thigh-length Walker Colt to an assortment of "ladies' pistols" suitable for concealing in a muff or small reticule. By the final quarter of the nineteenth century nearly every American owned a gun, with results similar to today's gun-control paranoia, as evidenced by the existence of anti-firearms ordinances in towns of all sizes from Abilene to the Barbary Coast. Surviving unposed photographs taken on the frontier yield very little in the way of exposed weapons.

Newspapers of the time contributed to this myth of law-lessness, concentrating, as the media will, on minor actions involving warring gangs at Tombstone's O.K. Corral and illegal ambushes by sworn officers of small-time criminals like Billy the Kid in New Mexico and a series of garish but quite lawful hangings of convicted murderers and rapists by Judge Isaac Parker at Fort Smith, Arkansas. Meanwhile the real battle for dominance was taking place almost unnoticed on the floor of Congress, where cattlemen who had fought the Indians for control of millions of acres of grassland fit for grazing but little else now confronted politicians determined to flood the prairie with farmers and votes. Although sporadic gunfights and lynchings in the disputed territories would culminate in the bloody Johnson County War of 1890, all the crucial victories and defeats would be recorded in the *Congressional Record.*

By 1890 the Indian was history, preserved in aspic on reservations—the inevitable casualty, like the buffalo and the open range, of creeping civilization. While it is tragic to mark the chain of broken promises and the caprice that governed his treatment, first as a sovereign nation, then as the enemy, finally as an ignorant orphaned child to be adopted and taught the white man's customs and practices, it is impossible to picture two such diverse cultures existing side by side, and as the Indian himself held as the way of things, the stronger tribe won. The end was ordained when the first red man spotted the sails of the first Spanish galleon rounding the earth's curve.

Buffalo, Indian, cowboy, and cavalryman—each made his entrance onto this hemisphere's largest stage, performed his part, and exited to make room for the next player. Considering the size and importance of these roles, one finds it hard to conceive why the prose minstrels of that day chose to ignore them in favor of the one-line walk-on assigned to that pilot fish of frontier chronology, the gunman.

They were an unwashed crew, these specialists trained in the quick and safe extinction of their fellow men to serve Mars and then turned loose on a nation torn in two and spliced together by threads of hate. Wars are traditionally followed by violent episodes. The shortsighted Reconstruction policies of a government left leaderless by assassination, together with the seeds of later land disputes hidden under the largesse of the Homestead Act and the lure of other men's gold in California and Nevada and Dakota, drew these killers by horse and stagecoach to tumbleweed towns whose very names, Tombstone and Deadwood and Cripple Creek, rang with doom.

They were uneducated, because there was better work for men of learning. (Doc Holliday, a dentist, was an exception, driven by tuberculosis to a death wish.) Lazy, because the pay was little enough for their work, which was never long in duration. If they pinned on a star, they might make as much as $150 a month plus fifty cents for every stray dog they shot inside city limits, or if they offered their services to cattlemen involved in range wars they might receive thirty and found for as long as the trouble lasted. But gunslinging lawmen drew trouble and few ranchers could afford to retain a hand who did nothing but wait for something to happen once the immediate danger was past, and so they drifted like predatory wolves with their noses into the wind for the scent of blood.

Experienced survivors, they avoided one another. No records exist to suggest that two gunmen of equal reputation ever faced each other in combat. When Hickok was marshal of Abilene, he and John Wesley Hardin met and agreed to stay apart for the duration of Hardin's stay. Those deadly fast-draw contests beloved of fiction, with chivalric rules and modes of accepted behavior, were unknown in a climate in which the man left standing by whatever means was considered the better of the pair. Most inquests were conducted on the spot by the nearest thing to law, and if the dead man was found to be armed, his fate was commonly attributed to self-defense, regardless of whether the fatal wound was in front or back.

With few exceptions these human scavengers lived briefly and died under sordid conditions from unexpected gunshots or in hastily fashioned nooses, their scant possessions auctioned off within hours of their deaths. Their lives and works were of no consequence in the larger history of the frontier and had a negligible effect on its outcome. Yet they were the first heroes recognized by an eastern establishment.

II. Art

Much if not all of the credit, or the blame, may be laid to one Edward Zane Carroll Judson, one of many self-styled colonels of that era who affected dubious commissions to gain a leg up in a society still gearing down from war. Although he had been a naval officer and had served with the army during the Seminole War, he claimed instead to have taken part in the siege of Montezuma during the war with Mexico. Under the pseudonym Ned Buntline he published a yellow sheet in New York City and invented the dime novel, through whose offices he quickly exhausted his own store of memoirs, real and imagined, and struck out west in search of new material.

An adulterer who married four times, he once shot a man to death in an argument over the man's wife, for which act he was hanged from an awning post and then cut down before he strangled. Small wonder that his scoundrel's heart was drawn toward unprincipled killers, whom he whitewashed and made over between yellow covers into defenders of the Golden Rule. The western novel's broadly advertised, rarely realized concern with Good vs. Evil may be traced directly to Buntline's potboilers. Like Thomas Mallory, himself a thorough blackguard best remembered for his Arthurian odes to Christian good conduct, Buntline made of his characters everything that he was not. In this manner he catapulted Wild Bill Hickok to national fame and spun Buffalo Bill Cody out of whole cloth and an obscure young apprentice scout given to alcoholic braggadocio.

The dime novel, reduced in price to a nickel following the development of more economical printing procedures, represents a gaudy evolutionary stop between the German horror pamphlet of the fifteenth century and the pulp magazine and paperback novel of our own recent history. Pounded out by a small army of prolific journalists under a staggering variety of colorful *noms de plume* and printed on coarse paper between shoddy bindings, the tracts fluttered like startled bats out of the publishing empires in New York and Chicago during the 1870s and 1880s and were the first items to sell in the millions of copies. That they were read to pieces and discarded in equally prodigious numbers is attested to by how few survive. Through them, Billy the Kid and the Jameses and Youngers and many more already mentioned rose to the prominence they still hold.

Firmly rooted in Victorian morality, the novels told stories of heroism in the face of blood-curdling odds that amused and bemused their subjects, astonished to find themselves mouthing temperance sermons and patriotic oaths whilst slaughtering savage Indians and highwaymen at Gatling-gun rate. The stories were devoured by schoolboys obliged to hide them beneath their mattresses at the sound of approaching parental footsteps, by immigrants laboriously teaching themselves English within tiny budgets, and by the heroes' own fellow frontiersmen, who in turn imitated the characters' dress and speech, wedding art and life in a self-fulfilling prophecy. Copies of *Beadle's Dime Library* and *Buffalo Bill Stories* appeared in bunkhouses in Wyoming and were found in hideouts hastily quit by bank and train robbers in Kansas and the Nations.

The importance of Buntline and his followers to frontier

history cannot be overstated. As its name suggests, "history" is not what happened, but what a small group of self-appointed spokesmen claim happened, and for all their stress on blood and black powder, an American West devoid of the Olympian heroes they created is impossible to feature.

Nor is it possible beyond a certain point to speculate upon whether the western novel as we know it would have developed at all but for these rude Homers. The epic chronologies of Virgil and Livy were no less distorted than *A History of the James Boys,* and further from their source. It is to these sagebrush scribes, therefore, that the author of this volume is ultimately indebted.

Although authenticity played a major role in selecting the titles that follow, none of them paints a completely accurate picture of the Old West. Complete accuracy is not the business of fiction. It is, however, the business of literary review, and apologies are offered in advance for whatever shortcomings the reader may discover in that vicinity.

1.

The Man with No Name

The Virginian (1902)

The western novel as it has come to be recognized sprang full-grown from the imagination of Owen Wister in 1902. In style and content, *The Virginian* owes little to the dime thrillers of Ned Buntline and Prentiss Ingraham and bears little resemblance to the more sanguinary, less sanguine "oaters" of a later day that are often and erroneously considered typical of the form. None of its heroes or villains is a professional gunman, not much blood is shed, and perhaps its most colorful character is a suicidal chicken named Em'ly. Yet, as is the pioneering privilege, it established most of the clichés with which Wister's literary heirs are still wrestling.

The Virginian is the road version of a drama that was playing out its final scenes even as the book went to press. Butch Cassidy and the Wild Bunch were still in flight from Pinkerton agents sworn to their death or capture. Jim Younger, released with his brother Cole from prison the previous year after serving a quarter-century for the robbery of the Northfield, Minnesota, bank, shot himself to death in St. Paul that autumn. Bat Masterson was writing sports copy in New York. Tom Horn, who helped talk Geronimo into surrendering, was gunning down suspected rustlers in Wyoming and had a year to live before hanging for a youth's murder. Meanwhile, employees of Thomas Edison were in New Jersey, scouting locations for a short motion picture to be called "The Great Train Robbery." The West stood poised somewhere between Wyatt Earp and John Wayne.

Enter Wister's nameless hero, a mysterious frontiersman with a pragmatic view of life founded on the philosophy that "a man has got to prove himself my equal before I'll believe him." Thus is born the proud man of action, whose opposite number, a rustler, back-shooter, and calumniator of women, represents the Devil. "Trampas has got hold of him," laments the Virginian, summing up the fate of a fellow cowboy who has gone over to the rustlers. From his famous first words to Trampas, "When you call me that, *smile!*" until the inevitable face-off—remarkable today for its subtlety and restraint—the line is drawn indelibly for Wister's successors to trace.

But the book is not all, nor even a tenth part, picturesque threats and spent powder. Beneath the surface hilarity of the Virginian's tale-telling contest with Trampas aboard the train to Medicine Bow, and of Em'ly, the demented hen who finds only a broken neck in her quest for motherhood, lie essential clashes of will and a regard for life that serious literature in our own day often promises and seldom delivers. Such episodes are part of a process by which the principals are constantly measuring themselves against one another on every level.

In Wister's hands, even the obligatory romance performs double duty, wooing the reader with a rough-hewn love story while hammering home the novel's basic theme, that West and East are totally alien worlds. Afternoon rides involving the hero and heroine, long since a staple of the form, become Socratic debates:

"All men are born equal," he now remarked slowly.
"Yes," she quickly answered, with a combative flash.
"Well?"

. . . "I used to have to learn about the Declaration of Independence. I hated books and truck when I was a kid."

"But you don't any more."

"No. I cert'nly don't. But I used to get kep' in at recess for
bein' so dumb. I was 'most always at the tail end of the class.
My brother, he'd be head sometimes."

"Little George Taylor is my prize scholar," said Molly.

. . . . "Who's last?"

"Poor Bob Carmody. I spend more time on him than on
all the rest put together."

"My!" said the Virginian. "Ain't that strange!"

. . . "I don't think that I understand you," said Molly,
stiffly.

"Well, it *is* mighty confusin'. George Taylor, he's your
best scholar, and poor Bob, he's your worst, and there's a lot
in the middle—and you tell me we're all born equal!"

Molly could only sit giggling in this trap he had so ingen-
iously laid for her.

The Virginian is not a western novel but a novel of the
West. Nowhere is this more apparent than in the brilliant
defense of lynch law presented by Judge Henry, the Virginian's employer, and in the easy camaraderie that exists between two captured rustlers and the men who will hang them
in the morning. Here, Wister's anonymous narrator (like the
Virginian, an unchristened Everyman in his own world), an
easterner, demonstrates his respect for and fear of an alien
code by spending a sleepless night in a cabin with the condemned men and refusing to interfere. Lesser artists, seething
with democratic outrage, have sought to press contemporary
eastern values on a period and a society that Wister knew too
well to attempt to influence. The reader, like the narrator,
is forever on the outside looking in.

The cowboy gunman is a myth. Ranch hands had little
time or inclination to practice their fast draw and less use for
it. Although to some extent Wister circumvents this stum-

bling-block by pitting two cowboys against each other in the climactic shootout—the first such in fiction—a potent whiff of tall tale lingers, and it is this larger-than-life element that has inspired several motion picture versions of the story and one long-running television series, the last inexplicably presenting Trampas and the Virginian as friends.

Much scholarly smoke has been blown on the subject of this particular Grendl, for reasons that are not quite clear. As a villain, Trampas is a rather bland foreshadowing of *Shane's* Mephistophelean Stark Wilson, and his worst crimes take place off the page. He stands as a mundane symbol of a greater evil, threatening an unspoken system of honor in a way no mere challenge between men can approach. If he lives, decency dies.

Readers accustomed to the superficial explicitness of the standard action western may be surprised by the aridity of Wister's prose, which forms a link between the allegorical sea stories of Joseph Conrad and Ernest Hemingway's deceptively flat narrative stance. It is not difficult to read in the way that William Faulkner is difficult to read, but it demands an alert mind, else much of its effect is lost. Whether this is a fault or a strength depends on which colors the literary fraternity is flying this season.

If the importance of a work is measured by the size of its audience, *The Virginian* stands taller than any dozen "straight" novels that have appeared since. But Wister's instinctive knowledge of the human condition remains the book's bedrock. By the time Trampas snarls, "I'll give you till sundown to leave town," the Virginian's reaction is not the knee-jerk of the so-called macho stereotype, but the inevitable response to a challenge of his entire concept of self.

2.

The Poet and the Pulpit

Riders of the Purple Sage (1912)

It has become fashionable in these more jaded times to denigrate Zane Grey, following the lead of critics who have never read him and writers seeking to promote their own interests by pulling down the old bull. This is symptomatic of the elevator-car philosophy of literature, whose fixed capacity demands that a passenger be turned out at each floor to make room for a new rider.

True, Grey's characters are punched out of the same grade of cardboard that new shirts come wrapped around. True, he borrows his plots from Victorian morality plays. He telegraphs his punches, mixes back-country dialect with the Queen's English, lingers over slight scenes in the manner of a starving dog licking a naked bone, while hurriedly dismissing key plot turns through a third party. But his books are read and reread by intelligent people in every country until the covers disintegrate. Owen Wister and Walter Van Tilburg Clark are held in awe; Zane Grey is loved.

Riders of the Purple Sage makes full use of Grey's poetic genius. Through his eyes, the Utah plain erupts into startling color and hidden valleys become paradises of virgin, aching beauty:

. . . . Around the red perpendicular walls, except under the great arc of stone, ran a terrace fringed at the cliff-base by

31

silver spruces; below that first terrace sloped another wider one densely overgrown with aspens, and the center of the valley was a level circle of oaks and alders, with the glittering green line of willows and cottonwood dividing it in half. Venters saw a number and variety of birds flitting among the trees. To his left, facing the stone bridge, an enormous cavern opened into the wall; and low down, just above the tree-tops, he made out a long shelf of cliff-dwellings he had seen—all ruins—had left him with haunting memory of age and solitude and of something past. He had come, in a way, to be a cliff-dweller himself, and those silent eyes would look down upon him, as if in surprise that after thousands of years a man had invaded the valley.

The narrative is divided between two heroes: Lassiter, a Mormon-baiting gunman whose determination to avenge his dead sister comprises the worst fears of nineteenth-century Gentiles regarding the polygamous sect; and Venters, a naïve former ranch hand who has dared to involve himself with a Mormon woman. The woman, Jane Withersteen, is a refreshing mix of subservience and sand, one of those plucky heroines who came so easily to Grey and who actually represent frontier womanhood far more accurately than the cursing feminists encountered in much of today's backlash western fiction.

None of these characters is the same by the story's close, events having softened Lassiter, hardened Venters, and shaken Jane from the Hamletlike indecision that keeps her vacillating between her conscience and her Mormon teachings. Only the villains, Elder Tull with his greedy eye on the Withersteen ranch and Bishop Dyer, the fanatical "proselytizer," go unreconstructed to their fates.

Riders knows many moments of unintentional humor. Lassiter's pursuit of Jane lacks the sharp philosophical seasoning of the Virginian's courtship, and Jane's attempt to woo the gunman into giving her his weapons, as she had done to Venters before him, would drive a Freudian whooping to his writing desk. Horses kneel camel-fashion for Jane to mount them. Lassiter heads off a stampede astride a blind stallion. Venters refuses a wounded young woman's request for food, asserting that it would be dangerous for her shoulder injury. And it is a rare reader who can swallow sweet little Fay's dialogue ("Muvver sended for oo . . . an' oo never tome") without retching. But the pace allows little time to dwell on these inadequacies, and for every fumble Grey provides at least two circus catches. "Oldrin's an honest thief," declares Lassiter at one point, surprising appreciative mirth out of his audience. The wry homily is a Grey trademark.

Readers in search of Grey at his most even should sample his grittily detailed study of the buffalo hunter's day-to-day existence in *The Thundering Herd* (1925) or experience the muted power of *The U.P. Trail* (1918), about the construction of the transcontinental railroad. But in neither of these comparatively disciplined efforts does he soar to the poetic heights of the descriptions in *Riders*.

Beyond them, what make the story a classic despite its shortcomings are his sure use of familiar stereotypes amid fairy-tale surroundings and his flair for pulse-pounding action. The last third of the book crackles with explosive climaxes, none more gripping than Venters' mountain race to catch Jerry Card, Tull's right bower:

> Cruelly he struck his spurs into Wrangle's flanks. A light touch of spur was sufficient to make Wrangle plunge. And now, with a ringing, wild snort, he seemed to double up in muscular convulsions and to shoot forward with an impetus that almost unseated Venters. The sage blurred by, the trail flashed by, and the wind robbed him of breath and hearing. . . . The giant sorrel thundered on—and on—and on. In every yard he gained a foot. He was whistling through his nostrils, wringing wet, flying lather, and as hot as fire. . . .

Zane Grey is not a "clever" writer, in that he never fails to deliver on a promise—one reason for his fans' fierce loyalty. They know that the villain will be punished, the hero will claim the heroine, and that in the process the storyteller will shed all artistic pretensions, roll up his sleeves, and go for the gut. Life should be so dependable and satisfying.

The Ox-Bow Incident (1940)

There are no eloquent Judge Henrys to speak for lynching in *The Ox-Bow Incident,* just the neanderthalic Deputy Sheriff Mapes and the sadistic Major Tetley, and thereby hangs Walter Van Tilburg Clark's grim tale of mob rule and the dark side of human nature.

Van Tilburg Clark draws a straighter, more predictable line than Wister, and yet, like Tetley himself, alternately extends and withdraws hope so that the reader is torn between faith in the accused rustlers' salvation and resignation to their fate. The narrative self-consciously avoids heroes. Davies, the most vocal opponent of the deed, is old and frail, symbolizing the impotence of reason amid high emotion. In an overlong soliloquy dominating the anticlimax, he confesses cowardice. Gerald Tetley, the Major's son and another wet blanket, whines and snivels throughout the story and hangs himself after the event. Even Gil and Art, the disinterested observers through whose eyes we follow the action, are guilty of noninvolvement.

A talky book, *Ox-Bow* moves slowly, choking on undigested lumps of unrealistic dialogue that make it resemble not so much the Old Testament tract it has often been compared to, as Greek allegory. Intones Gerald Tetley:

"Oh, we're smart," he said, the same way. "It's the same

thing," he cried; "all we use it for is power. Yes, we've got
them scared all right, all of them, except the tame things
we've taken the souls out of. We're the cocks of the dungheap,
all right; the bullies of the globe."

Intended as the book's conscience, young Tetley is Lear's
hyperperceptive Fool without the latter's sense of irony. But
he is just one inhabitant of a remote community seemingly
blessed with the gift of articulation. Everyone is an orator.
Even Monty Smith, the drunken lout who personifies the
worst emotions of the party, experiences remarkably little
difficulty with his vocabulary and syntax. Van Tilburg
Clark's tin ear is the book's major flaw.

Its one formidable strength is an explosive admixture of
stick-figure characters, laid with the skill of a demolitions
expert to go off in the places and times where it will wreak
the most havoc on the reader's sensibilities. Published the
year France fell to Hitler's Wehrmacht, its concern with
modern fascism overwhelms its token nod to period, and
from the presence of an unjustly accused trio to its progres-
sive, suffocating sense of doom the book bears a suspicious
resemblance to Humphrey Cobb's World War I classic, *Paths
of Glory*. In spite of this and the burden of an undeveloped
subplot involving a gossip-ruined woman come back with
a new husband (the author's indecision over which psychological cancer-spots to expose is at its most irritating here),
Ox-Bow climbs inexorably down an ever-darkening shaft
and reveals its worst truth in a blinding flash at the bottom.
When Davies in his desperation to prove Martin's innocence
approaches Art with the condemned man's letter to his wife,
neither Art nor the reader wants to know what it says. Van
Tilburg Clark has pointed his finger, and it isn't at the guy
standing behind us.

3.

Three Consecutive Knights

Shane (1949)

He was clean-shaven and his face was lean and hard and burned from high forehead to firm, tapering chin. His eyes seemed hooded in the shadow of the hat's brim. He came closer, and I could see that this was because the brows were drawn in a frown of fixed and habitual alertness. Beneath them the eyes were endlessly searching from side to side and forward, checking off every item in view, missing nothing. As I noticed this, a sudden chill, I could not have told why, struck through me there in the warm and open sun.

In the above passage, coming near the end of a two-and-a-half-page descriptive opening that would know the blue pencil of any of the apprentice editors usually entrusted with western fiction at today's publishing houses, Jack Schaefer applies the final brush-strokes to the mythic American hero. There is a little of Christ and George Washington in this small, wistfully sad package, spared the Virginian's anonymity only by a one-syllable name that sounds like wind in the lonely grass.

People who "never read westerns" have read *Shane*. Its deceptively simple storyline and well-used cattleman-vs.-homesteader theme have attracted more readers from outside the genre than any other work. The reasons are all caught up in our revolutionary past.

Much of the book's stature lies in its narrative approach. From the low angle of a small boy's eyes, the principals tower against a vast Wyoming sky, forging something Homeric out of a situation as prosaic as two men laboring to uproot a large tree-stump. The scene reflects the Man-against-Nature conflict that stands ageless and unchanging beyond the ephemeral stuff of men popping firearms at one another. But those firearms are big enough for a boy, becoming things of wicked beauty:

> . . . It was black, almost blue black, with the darkness not in the enamel but in the metal itself. The grip was clear on the outer curve, shaped to the fingers on the inner curve, and two ivory plates were set into it with exquisite skill, one on each side.
>
> The smooth invitation of it tempted your grasp. I took hold and pulled the gun out of the holster. It came so easily that I could hardly believe it was there in my hand. Heavy like father's, it was somehow much easier to handle. You held it up to aiming level and it seemed to balance itself into your hand.

Smooth and sinister like his weapon, Shane is the spark that touches off Schaefer's powder keg. Luke Fletcher, the cattle baron bent on driving the farmers off his range, supplies the powder, gunman Stark Wilson the fuse. Much has been made of Wilson as evil personified, but it is an impersonal evil compared to the insinuating influence of Trampas in *The Virginian,* albeit one more overtly dangerous. He is mettle enough for Shane, at any rate, through whom Schaefer says again and again that dangerous men attract danger and cannot escape their past. How he says it is the key to the book's power.

Marian Starrett, although she remains faithful to and in love with her homesteading husband Joe, is attracted to the aura of mystery and peril that surrounds Shane. He is responsive but reserved, without exhibiting the absurd bash-fulness of Lassiter toward Jane Withersteen in *Riders of the Purple Sage;* Shane's reservation stems from his friendship with Starrett, not from inexperience with women. His first weeks with the family are a paradise in which the serpent, Wilson, has yet to rear its head. His gun is stored away and he has exchanged his city clothes for homespun. But the deteriorating situation with the cattlemen, punctuated by Shane's fistfight with Fletcher's man Chris, soon has him wrestling with his own nature:

> . . . Shane was changed. He tried to keep things as they had been with us and on the surface nothing was different. But he had lost the serenity that had seeped into him through the summer. He would no longer sit around and talk with us as much as he had. He was restless with some far hidden desperation.

When first encountered, Shane is observed pausing at a fork in the road near Starrett's farm, "studying the choice." He makes it, but it is ultimately the wrong one for him. This is the book's central problem, and once it is resolved, the obligatory shootout with Wilson is almost anticlimactic. The real climax occurs when Marian Starrett announces: "Oh, Joe, can't you see what I'm talking about? I don't mean what you've done to Chris. I mean what you've done to Shane."

The reading public will allow a writer only one classic, and while in many ways Jack Schaefer's *Monte Walsh* is a better western than *Shane*—there are those who will argue that in scope, authenticity, and unexpressed emotion *Walsh* is the finest ever written—the stark yet lyric subtlety of the more famous work assigns it a permanent spot on the ele-vator-car of American literature. As an icon it has often been equaled. It can never be surpassed.

Hondo (1953)

Borrow *Shane*'s recipe: A saddle-wise loner with a scarlet past, a homesteading family with a small boy, a threat from without. Remove one of the moral obstacles by making the father a lowlife and absenting him from much of the story, but replace it with a bigger one by forcing the hero to kill him in self-defense, so that dead he endangers the hero's relationship with the mother more than he could have alive. Deposit this disturbing psychological triangle in a desert crawling with hostile Apaches, call it *Hondo,* and make room for another figure in the brisk pantheon of fine western storytellers.

Probably, Louis L'Amour took no such cold-blooded approach to his masterpiece, but the parallels are there, and help to explain its enduring appeal. As with Shane, the reader meets Hondo Lane alone on horseback. But the nonobjective omniscient narration is less intrusive than that of Schaefer's young Bob Starrett:

> He was a big man, wide-shouldered, with the lean, hard-boned face of the desert rider. There was no softness in him. His toughness was ingrained and deep, without cruelty, yet quick, hard, and dangerous. Whatever wells of gentleness might lie within him were guarded and deep.

We are thus forewarned that something will happen to open those "wells of gentleness." Schaefer's come-to-realize method is more subtle, but never touches L'Amour's ability—give or take a distracted echoing of the phrase "and deep"—to catalogue a man's character along with his appearance without belaboring the point.

Unlike Shane, whose sense of being out of his element provides the nerve center of his story, Hondo is very much a man of his world, as indistinguishable from the savage landscape as his buckskin shirt and faded jeans are from the desert tans that surround them. Angie Lowe and her son Johnny, eking an existence out of a ranch squarely in the Apaches' warpath, are the outsiders. The stranger takes them in hand to show them his world as the Starretts invited their stranger to learn theirs. Throughout the book, Sam, Hondo's half-wild mongrel (long since a familiar device), represents his master's situation on a less complex level, reluctantly accepting a semblance of domestication while retaining his uncivilized identity. Dying with an Apache lance through his body, the dog tries to lick Angie's hand, uncovering wells of his own.

Hondo's Stark Wilson is Silva, hot-tempered heir apparent to the aging Mescalero chief Vittoro. But for Ed Lowe, Angie's aptly named no-account husband, Silva is the sole personal evil in a cataclysm that for its setting has all the impersonal inevitability of a natural disaster. The tension before the storm drives the narrative at a breakneck pace, with Hondo appointing himself lightning-rod. Vittoro's death and Silva's ascension signal the cloudburst. L'Amour sets up the metaphorical with the literal:

> . . . And then came the rain and the wind. It struck with a solid blow. There was an instant of pause, then the downpour. Thunder roared in the distance, then lightning snapped at the ridge to his right and there was a smell of brimstone and charred grass.

This is the planting rain, by which time Angie must decide which of Vittoro's bucks to take for a mate. In the larger sense, it is a symbol of the greater tempest to follow.

Within the confines of a formula often scorned for its simplicity, L'Amour manipulates with sure hands the traces of the greater plot and of the hero's moral dilemma regarding the woman he has made a widow. The result is a rich, fast-

moving chronicle of men and women caught in a collision
of conflicting values. If it could not have been written but
for *Shane,* the author has more than repaid his debt to western
literature.

Louis L'Amour has never written anything to compare
with his first novel, although *High Lonesome, Flint,* and *The
First Fast Draw* are beyond the talents of many of his most
critical colleagues. The plot discrepancies in *The Iron Marshal,* the stultifying aimlessness of *Bendigo Shafter,* the bland
characterization that makes fool's gold of *Comstock Lode*
are poor clay for the creator of Hondo Lane. For all its shortcomings the pulp school that produced Max Brand and Luke
Short would never have armed a hero with a Winchester
repeater in 1859 or allowed a backwoodsman to use "ain't"
and "to whom" in the same sentence, as L'Amour does in
Lode. But the pulp school never produced a *Hondo.*

The Shootist (1975)

Glendon Swarthout's *The Shootist* takes place in a crowded
West with no room for Shanes and Hondos, viewed through
a soiled veil of exhaustion and death and stinking black-powder smoke. Where Shane considered his own obsolescence
with wry approval, John Bernard Books, a gunman preparing for his last showdown, glowers at it with dark philosophy. Having just read of the death of Queen Victoria,

> He thought: Well, Victoria, Your Royal Highness, old
> lady, old girl, we are about to get together. I will not make
> as big a splash as you did. I do not expect they will sell much
> drape, but there may be a minute of silence in the saloons.
> I have never read what a man is supposed to do when he is
> presented to you. Kiss your hand, I imagine. But you will
> know a gent when you meet him, you will recognize blood

as blue in a way as yours. I will show you my guns, if you like, and we will drink tea and talk. You were the last of your kind, and they say . . . that I am the last of mine, so we have a hell of a lot in common.

Having cheated the black-powder death of his era, Books faces the bleaker death of cancer, its twentieth-century replacement. He is Shane stripped of his illusions, forsaking the open skies of Schaefer's West for a cramped coffin of a room in an El Paso boarding house. Swarthout's choice of setting, the tight airless stairwells and drab papered walls that make today's tourists wonder at the resolution of the pioneers when they visit buildings of the period, narrows his focus, sparing no detail of one man's slightly stale tragedy. The claustrophobic effect of *The Ox-Bow Incident* is here carried to its inevitable extreme. The blustering judges and sanctimonious clergymen, figures of fun in Van Tilburg Clark's tale and in *The Virginian,* have taken over. Books's Angie Lowe, a widow named Rogers, is raising a son no better than Ed Lowe. Trapped in a tunnel of indifference with death at both ends, Books chooses the one he recognizes.

Few will mourn. Not Thibodo, El Paso's marshal, for whom the prospect of an electrified trolley holds more interest than the last chapter of a forgotten history playing itself out within his jurisdiction; or Dobkins, an exploitative journalist hoping to enrich himself, like the barber and the undertaker and the liveryman, from Books's long-overdue death; or Serepta, the woman Books loved, and who in the final extremity proves herself a whore in spirit as well as profession. The process that begins with the condemned man violating his promise to himself not to seek pity and ends with him selling his guns and his shorn hair and his own corpse includes the surrender of every romantic conception he retains coming into the story. No one lies to a dead man.

One of Swarthout's more mannered techniques, the clinical

description of what happens when lead meets flesh and arteries and bone, indicates the completeness of his realism:

> . . . The bullet was fired from above and from the rear, an oblique trajectory, at a range of seven feet. It penetrated the temporal bone above and forward of the ear, exposing the brain, passing through the brain, carrying with it segments of skull, and exited through the right orbit, or eye socket, taking off the ethmoid plate and the bridge of the nose. . . .

By eschewing Wister's restraint and Grey's distance, the author here rips away the last romantic veil. Often brutal, sometimes self-conscious, but always compelling, *The Shootist* remains as real as gray-matter on a barroom floor.

4.

Beef

The Sea of Grass (1936)

If the capacity to view an old conflict from the unpopular side indicates maturity, then the literature of the American West has attained full growth, at least in the matter of the feuds between cattlemen and homesteaders that scarred this country's long adolescence. Half a century before *Shane,* the revolutionary fixation dictated that because the farmers and small ranchers were outmanned and outgunned by the barons who tamed the wilderness,they must be seen as heroic Davids to Big Cattle's Goliath. Thus, *Shane*'s Luke Fletcher and *Duel in the Sun*'s Senator McCanles became despotic anach-ronisms preying upon the weak and treading on the toes of Progress.

The Great Depression and the southwestern dust bowl of the 1930s temporarily altered this perspective. In *The Sea of Grass,* Conrad Richter lays much of the blame for those related disasters on the bull shoulders of the nesters who tore up and pulverized the western grasslands into floury dust to be lifted and blown away by the prairie winds. A dozen years before Schaefer returned the laurels to these shortsighted stal-warts, Richter's Nick Carraway-like Hal Brewton sees them "barking and snapping around my uncle's legs like a pack of dogs."

His uncle is Colonel Brewton, monarch over an area larger than Massachusetts and Connecticut, wrested by blood from the Indians and put to the whip and the spur to feed a hungry growing nation on beef, now forced by changing times in general and Judge Brice Chamberlain in particular to relinquish his claim, first by inches, then by tens of miles to the thickening horde from the East. Through it all, he retains mythic stature:

> . . . moving erect and towering down the crowded aisle along the wall, a familiar, proud, almost insolent figure in a long gray broadcloth coat with tails and bulging on the side toward us with what I knew was a holster capped with ivory handles, his coal-black eyebrows and moustache white with alkali dust, and in the abrupt quiet of the room the fall of his boot-heels like the shots of a pistol.

But as the elements ravage a land denuded by plow and harrow, so an ignorant government in Washington and an unwashed rabble presented as little more than human rodents gnaw away at a proud countenance already undermined by personal tragedy. Land and man are one and doomed, yet both survive, like the huge cottonwood standing off Salt Fork's plaza—struck by lightning, its bark eaten away by nesters' stock, but that "still stood there green and cool, sheltering . . . all who passed under its branches or pulled chairs into its broad shade."

A prose poem, *The Sea of Grass* laments within a remarkably short span of pages the twenty-year decline of the great ranches before an eastern onslaught here typified by Judge Chamberlain's arrogant bearing and vain blond locks. But it is a story too of a love lost. Gone is Lutie, a breath of delicate scent from St. Louis who swept in, touched the Colonel and all around her, then fluttered back to the " 'stores and lights and music and things going on.' " The words, however, belong to Brock Brewton, ostensibly one of the Colonel's three children by Lutie but probably Chamberlain's bastard son. As seen by Hal, himself having outgrown his boots and chaps and taken up medicine, Brock combines his mother's basic shallowness with his true father's moral weakness into a career in crime that ends with him bleeding to death in an abandoned nester's shack, smirking at a framed newspaper print of Christ in the manger. He is the promise of a new frontier gone sour in the face of change.

Change is the story's theme. Viewed through the mist of decades, *The Sea of Grass* bears no little resemblance to Gogol's bittersweet dirge for another dead frontier in another hemisphere in *Taras Bulba*. Remembers Hal:

> And that night as I lay in my sleepless bunk staring into the white haze that entered my deep window, I fancied that in the milky mist I could see the prairie as I had seen it all my life and would never see it again, with the grass in summer sweeping my stirruped thighs and prairie chickens scuttling ahead of my pony; with the ponds in fall black and noisy with waterfowl, and my uncle's seventy thousand head of cattle rolling in fat; with the tracks of endless game in the winter snow and thousands of tons of wild hay cured and stored on the stem; and when the sloughs of the home range greened up in the spring, with the scent of warming wet earth and swag after swag catching the emerald fire, with horses shedding and snorting and grunting as they rolled, and everywhere the friendly indescribable solitude of that lost sea of grass.

In Richter's hands, the war for possession of a diminishing prairie becomes a song of memory and innocence plowed under by blind Progress. He sings of creatures and concerns not fading and curling in dusty archives but flushed with stubborn life. Yet each lyric is released reluctantly and with the constant reminder that all of these things are irretrievably, achingly gone.

Monte Walsh (1963)

One of the more evil blessings a sardonic Fate may grant a writer is the first-novel classic. Critics caught unprepared at the time of its appearance will rally to apply it as a yardstick to his later work, and any advances he may make in style and vision will be swamped in the popular groundswell from the earlier effort. Such is the case with Jack Schaefer's towering *Monte Walsh,* in every way a superior book to *Shane,* but still out of print in a time when every western rack of any size is certain to yield a crisp new copy of his first novel.

Monte Walsh is an odyssey in time, following its cowboy hero from adolescence to old age through the growth and death of the open range and the cattle industry's passage from heroic individualism to corporate nonentity. Everyman, Walsh never rises above the level of common cowboy, managing instead to carve out his own legend among his peers as "a good man with a horse," the very best that can be said of one in his profession. Much of the story's poetic beauty, in fact, resides in its celebration of the prosaic. The Rites of Passage chronicle both a boy's growth to manhood and the development of an American national character:

> Knock off a few years fast. Let a boy emerge as a man, age in the years unimportant but the seasoning yes, a young one absorbing the skills of a trade, of a way of life, of an attitude toward existence. Maybe it will add up to something, if only to a grasp on one of many like him, separate only in the small fragments of individuality, who shared that trade, that way of life, in a time and a place, a short time but a big place, a wisp of eternity across a third of a continent.

Organic but not without structure, the story plays events grand and small off its hero like the flicker of sheet lightning off an indestructible rock face. Now he is a rebellious boy

honing his destiny in the yowling infant cattle trade, now
an old man urging his horse in a rainstorm down a greasy
mountain path too primitive for the fragile early automobiles
that would render those skills frivolous. Here is Hellfire, the
quintessential horse that couldn't be rode, come at last to
loggerheads with Walsh, the fabled cowboy that couldn't be
throwed; Chet Rollins, partner in a hundred roundups and
line camps, one of the last to trade in his rope and spurs for
a career in business, leaving Walsh the last; the Slash Y, a
brand whose wranglers belong to a group so elite that young
Lon Hall, dying of injuries received in a spill while fleeing
a band of rustlers, can say: "Well, anyways, I was Slash Y
for a while."

The book is as episodic as the cowboy's life, cohered by
only an attitude and Schaefer's omniscient voice speaking
from the smoky distance of later wisdom, sweeping across
seasons and miles and pausing to linger on such poignancies
as Yellow-Hair Hattie, everyone's night woman for a price
but Walsh's for himself, though the thing is never spoken
until she dies, a casualty of her profession. "Goddamn it,"
he eulogizes. "And she made a man of me. What there is of
me." The one fixed point in a changing West (the phrase
"A man and a horse" recurs most frequently throughout the
book, and always refers to Walsh and his mount of the moment), he notes its arrivals and departures like Richter's hoary
cottonwood.

But like the cottonwood, destined to fall. Good men die
in this demythologized West, not necessarily like Shane, riding into a figurative sunset bleeding from a possibly mortal
wound, but just as heroically, of pneumonia acquired during
a flood rescue and damaged lungs earned years earlier fighting
a prairie fire. Broken John Henry-like by his duel with creeping technology, Walsh dies, and with him ends Jack Schaefer's heart-swelling and tragic but ultimately triumphant epic
poem. Chet Rollins' instructions to the stonecutter who will

chisel Walsh's marker might have been voiced by the ghosts of the faceless, leather-lean generations of horsemen who powered Shaefer's pen: "Cut it deep. I want it to last. I want it to outlast any of us. And our kids. And our kids' kids."

Sam Chance (1965)

Change has concerned the best western writers. In 1879, the year Billy the Kid came to national infamy in the Lincoln County War, Thomas Alva Edison forced electricity through a loop of carbonized cotton thread in a vacuum, inventing the incandescent lamp; and the untamed West knew the first chill of death. The cross-purposes of civilization and wilderness and their inevitable outcome course like Edison's current through Benjamin Capps's *Sam Chance,* a novel of the men who built the cattle industry.

No Colonel Brewton, Sam Chance accepts and at times invites change. Not for him to go on fighting a lost War for Southern Independence, he cuts his horse out of the string captured from his regiment by the Union Army, sells his farm in western Tennessee, and strikes out for Texas to help invent the business of rounding up wild longhorns for sale to a hungry postwar nation. Although he has fought Indians and hanged rustlers for the land and his stock, he doesn't begrudge the Richteresque nesters who push in later their fair use of his range and donates much of his own deeded property for the construction of a town (and later, of a cemetery) whose residents will resent his hard-won riches and stack a new legislature against him. He embraces barbed wire and lends his own ranch hands to the task of building and maintaining roads. But his foresight is ignored, his motives misunderstood:

The gift of the cemetery to the town might have been considered a peace offering if any person had thought of it that way. It might have been thought that the old man was saying, "Here, lay your precious dead beside mine. Let the pioneers of the '80s and the pioneers of the '60s rest together." But not even Chance thought of that. He had the impulse, so he made the offer; they could accept the land or turn it down. He didn't give a damn.

The townspeople were certainly not inclined to think kindly of the act. They said, "What's ten acres to a bullionaire like that?" Or, "He just wants the town to take care of his private burying ground"; this in spite of his continuing to care for the place after the deed had changed hands. Or, "He's kicked the poor people around all his life; now he just wants to ease his conscience."

He fares hardly better with lawmakers and the press, who treat him at first with Judaean hostility and finally, when it is too late to matter, as a quaint relic of less enlightened days. But by then he has outgrown them all.

On a human level, it is the familiar story of a man raising a family that will eventually care for him in his last infirmity as a parent for his child. Like Brewton, Chance loses his wife to the harsh prairie; but while Lutie leaves of her own will, Martha Chance ages ahead of her years and dies. In time she is laid to rest in Tennessee at her request—her world, but a place, in the words of son Peter, "so far away from home." Too demanding for southern female stock, the ranch remains home for the son who grows up to run it and the daughter who, widowed by another of those wars Chance has outgrown, returns to it to nurse her father. The life is in the blood.

This much Chance knows, and on the last day of his life he cuts himself free of a new century's traces and rides out to die on his range, reliving in his mind the gone times and dreaming of a future not so very much unlike the one that has become his past. His body is discovered in a dry buffalo wallow with his horse grazing nearby and his old .22 rifle at his side. He has expired on the Texas prairie, in the end the only acquaintance that understands him.

The Day the Cowboys Quit (1971)

The end of the western cattle industry's feudal ways had not so much to do with eastern legislation and unexpected natural disasters as with the erosion of trust. This is the peg on which Elmer Kelton hangs *The Day the Cowboys Quit,* and in his hardened craftsman's hands it is a strong one. Corruption begins with something as seemingly innocuous as the posting of rules already long observed among cowboys along the Canadian River setting, spreads when the order comes down forbidding ranch hands to own cattle, and finishes with the cowboys voting against the men to whom they have sworn fealty, a devastating turn and one that will eventually destroy the natural order.

The unlikely leader of this rebellion is Hugh Hitchcock, the most faithful of the cowboys assembled. This Hamlet's loyalty to a rather unworthy Charlie Waide, who bows to the humiliating regulations demanded by his fellow ranchers, is constantly at odds with his duties to his cowboy peers. Scattered evidence of disrespect among his hands places Waide in favor of broadsiding rules of conduct—a slap in the face to cowhands who have observed them for years without being asked—and when one of his own men, the ironically christened Law McGinty, is found to be a rustler, he throws in with martinet Prosper Selkirk and the other bean-counting ranchers to outlaw private herds among ranch employees. Apologizes Kelton:

Charlie Waide knew the cow. But he found himself ill at ease among a new kind of ranchers who knew cows as figures on a ledger rather than flesh and blood creatures of leg and long horn; who thought of a herd of cattle as a large sum written in black at the bottom of a page rather than as a teeming mass of bawling beasts, strung majestically across a mile or more of God's green grass, the brown dust rising and swirling above them like some living thing, the air sharp with the bite of hoof-flung dirt and the mingled smells of trampled green grass and calves' milky breath and fresh manure.

To Hitchcock he confides, "I felt like a crippled horse penned up amongst a pack of gray lobo wolves. I was fishin' in deep waters against that crew."

Reluctantly, "Hitch" joins the strike against the new restrictions, but the method is ahead of its time and embers out amid petty demands for impossible wages and the cowboys' own impatience. But it leaves its mark, and when the triumphant ranchers retaliate by seizing the small herds, Hitch's among them, and lynching Law McGinty in the act, the epitaph for a way of life is etched in hemp and black powder.

Along the way Kelton passes comment on the culture whose dissolution he is tracing. Although it seems inappropriate to label him a master of the novel of manners, his life-earned knowledge of the cattleman's existence shines brightest in his commentary on range etiquette, as when Hitch questions himself heretically why it is so important that the cowboy rise before dawn, and when he demonstrates values unique to his work:

Hitch always recalled that Dayton Brumley was riding a Figure 4 sorrel called Blaze for the crooked streak that ran from forelock down to a snip nose. Blaze had fox ears and three stocking feet and an R Slash branded on his left hip, and moved with as smooth a saddle gait as Hitch ever saw.

He forgot in later years just what Dayton Brumley looked like. After all that time a man couldn't be expected to remember details.

The somewhat enigmatic Lafey Dodge symbolizes the archaisms left stranded by the outgoing tide. Seen at first as an evil on the scale of Trampas and Stark Wilson, he is by story's end a dinosaur, ignorant of his approaching extinction and adhering to a code as antiquated as the cowboy's violated oath. Hitch, elected sheriff in an act of true rebellion against the lords of the range, watches the gunman ride off into obsolescence with something akin to pity.

The erosion that began at the top eats its way down, even to Hitch, who goes through the motions of hair-branding a stray calf from another ranch so that no one else can claim it before it's old enough to wear his brand. That he decides at the moment of truth not to go through with it is as irrelevant as his courtship of McGinty's widow; what matters is that his faith in the cowboy's creed is shaken. As do all the half-remembered men who people *The Day the Cowboys Quit,* the lame old bulls who built their fortunes from the saddle and the tailcoated easterners who inherited them and the loud, profane, dust-eating wranglers who made those fortunes possible on twenty and found and a coil of rope, he has answered Waide's early question: "Can you, Hitch? Can anybody guarantee anything any more?"

5.

The Greasy Grass

A Civil War battlefield promotion to the rank of brevet-brigadier general at age 23 and a disputed winter victory over the Cheyennes at the Washita earned him an annotation in the record of the conquest of the frontier. But on June 25, 1876, this unpopular commander, distrusted by his own men and despised by his superiors in Washington, led five troops of cavalry into a valley known to Indians as the Greasy Grass and became, next to Napoleon Bonaparte, the most written-about military leader in history.

Recently, revisionist historians have sought to play down as a minor action what happened to George Armstrong Custer and his Seventh Cavalry on that blistering day on Montana's High Plains. Yet it prolonged the Indian wars fourteen years, devastated the United States centennial celebration in Philadelphia, and enlivens many a soporific cocktail party today. Speculation, that lodestone of successful historical fiction, is immeasurably richer.

No Survivors (1950)

Selecting his material from history and his own imagination, Will Henry has erected a Parthenon of western lore and scraped the dust of decades from its icons. *No Survivors,* possibly the keystone in his American Indian frieze, represents the "docudrama" technique, forged by Sir Walter Scott and now very much a mainstay of prime-time television, at its most effective. Although history tells us that no white men survived the Battle of the Little Big Horn, the number of writers who have brought forth their own witnesses raises questions about how Custer managed to lose the fight with so many men at his command. Henry pioneers this premise with John Clayton, a former Confederate officer captured by the Sioux and educated in tribal custom, who is present the day the author of a successful *Galaxy* series on the plains tribes leads 215-225 men (few chronologists agree on the actual number) against a village of upwards of 6,000 subjects of his study.

Clayton alone survives the Fetterman massacre of 1866 and spends the next decade assimilating himself into Sioux society, only to be marked for death by his former Indian friends when he confides his desire to return to the white world. Ironically, that same white world distrusts him for a renegade, and it is as a prisoner that he accompanies Custer and the Seventh Cavalry to the Little Big Horn. This warrior bird with clipped wings thus fulfills the unspoken prophecy of his Sioux name—Cetan, or Walking Hawk. One of the more labored contrivances of this first Henry novel involves Clayton's penchant for being raised from the dead, twice his fate before his third resurrection by a forgiving Chief Crazy Horse when he is discovered still breathing among the Seventh's slain.

Patiently, like an American H. Rider Haggard, Henry backs and fills his story, employing fact upon fact to shore up weak spots in what is on the face of it an insupportable assumption—that the same man lived through both of the U.S. Cavalry's greatest massacres—before the reader can fix on them. While enthralling, this approach is sometimes hampered by the inclusion of undigested lumps of pure history, both in the body of the tale and in lengthy footnotes, making one wonder if he is reading a novel or a textbook. Also,

Henry's insistence upon telling more than is necessary about a character or about an offhand historical reference in dialogue leads to such gaffes as a gratuitous mention of Buffalo Bill Cody and Wild Bill Hickok years before the pair acquired their famous nicknames. We are thus made observers of rather than participants in history, and not an entirely accurate one at that. Wister's lyrical/philosophical view of a vanishing world can survive such fudging; Henry's deadly chronological one is seriously impaired.

But Clayton's larger-than-life quality overcomes all doubts, sweeping his audience along with him through the holocaust of the Indian wars astride Hussein, a mean but faithful gelding by the Virginian's Monte out of Venters' Wrangle. Life among the savages, touched on only casually and in retrospect in *Hondo*, is the superstructure of *No Survivors*, in which Henry closely examines the day-to-day existence of the Sioux two decades before Thomas Berger discovers the Cheyenne in his own squaw-man-survives-Custer saga, *Little Big Man*. Clayton manifests none of the ambivalence he feels toward such white leaders as Colonel Carrington and Custer in his conversations with Chief Crazy Horse, whom he unabashedly venerates. But the Noble Red Man conceit is not for Henry, who cynically relates the other warriors' ability to turn their backs on Clayton the moment he proposes returning to civilization. In a scene preceding that turn, the Indian-as-petulant-child motif anticipates Thomas Berger's *Little Big Man*:

> . . . It was a time for dainty treading.
> "Yellow Bird, is there any question who are the greatest?"
> "None, the Sioux of course."
> . . . "Fine. Will the Sioux then argue like squaws as to who shall ride first in a thing which is squaw's work in the first place?"
> "Never."
> "Who shall ride first, then?"

"The Sioux, of course."

I could see that we had missed connections somewhere. Another tack was in order.

"Very well. And suppose Three Stars tricks us, coming up behind while we travel? Will the Sioux then be able to explain to Dull Knife why they ride where the safety is? Do you want Hump and Little Wolf to fight your battles?"

"Not while I breathe."

"Who rides first, then?"

"The Cut Arms. It could never be any other way. Surely you can see that, Cetan? How could it be otherwise?"

"You are right, Yellow Bird. Your mind is as clear as a trout's eye. It is a wonder I had not seen you were right all along."

"You are sometimes very ignorant, Cetan."

The scene is reminiscent of the Virginian's verbal duels with Molly. Henry's slyly intellectual humor, bordering on the satirical, helps to remove the onus from his hero's talent for miraculously surviving the reports of his own death.

A master of gut-wrenching acton, Henry injects the Little Big Horn fight with an urgency that makes the reader eager in spite of his own foreknowledge to learn its outcome. Henry and his protagonist Clayton blow hot and cold on the notion of George Armstrong Custer as Great Man, but the awesome waste of war regardless of who is victor overlays the last quarter of *No Survivors* like dust on the Seventh's guidon.

Whether it bears the Clay Fisher label (*Yellowstone Kelly*, many others) or the more famous pseudonym, a Will Henry title lends integrity to any rack overstocked with Louis L'Amour's lesser work and the hackery of the "Adult Western."

Little Big Man (1964)

Thomas Berger's refusal to cleave to any single genre has cost him the good will of critics frustrated by their inability to assign him a convenient pigeonhole. While this practice often denies him the insight gained through repeated exploration, in *Little Big Man* his lack of prolonged exposure to the western form leads to refreshing results.

Borrowing his basic concept and attitude from *No Survivors*, he covers much of the same ground in recounting Jack Crabb's adventures from his childhood among the Cheyennes to the Little Big Horn, but broadens the scope to admit a celebrity cast headed by Wild Bill Hickok and including cameo appearances by Wyatt Earp and Calamity Jane. Along the way, Crabb touches all the bases one man can in the frontier experience, becoming Indian brave, gunfighter, cardsharp, town drunk, and scout before destiny places him, like Henry's John Clayton, in both camps at Custer's Last Stand. Berger meanwhile indulges in some myth-busting with the aid of his garrulous hero:

> . . . "I reckon you must know Wild Bill purty well, to bother him at a time like this."
>
> "Don't know him a-tall," says I, "and don't know as I want to. What makes him so important?"
>
> This fellow says: "You never heard how he took care of the McCanles gang ten years ago at the Rock Crick stage station down in Jefferson County? There was six of them, I believe, and they come for Wild Bill, and he took three with his hands, two with his bowie, and just beat the other to death with a gunstock."
>
> I immediately reduced that by half in my mind, for I had been on the frontier from the age of ten and knew a thing as to how fights are conducted. When you run into a story of more than three against one and one winning, then you have

heard a lie. I found out later I was right in this case: Wild Bill killed only McCanles and two of his partners, and all from ambush.

Life with the Cheyennes was subtly different from Sioux ways, and the differences are detailed, suggesting that Berger does not depend as heavily on Henry's research as some have charged. He is also treading firmer ground historically, as it was the Cheyennes and not the Sioux who were known regularly to take in strays. Berger avoids his predecessor's hero-worship, presenting Old Lodge Skins, the chief who adopts Crabb and names him Little Big Man, as a comic figure who displays his nobility in ways less obvious than Henry's Crazy Horse-as-Christ. The childish petulance of the untutored savage, introduced by Henry, is seized by Berger and borne to Hellerian heights when Crabb misguidedly employs logic in an attempt to prove his identity to a skeptical brave:

> Burns Red in the Sun said: "He rode beside me at the Battle of the Long Knives, where the white men did not know how to fight. He was killed there after rubbing out many bluecoats. But the white men did not get his body. He turned into a swallow and flew away across the bluffs."
>
> "I tell you," I cried, "that I am Little Big Man. How would I know about him otherwise?"
>
> "All people know of him," said Burns Red in that stubborn redskin manner. "He is a great hero of the Human Beings. Everybody knows the Human Beings, so everybody would know of him. I shall not talk of this further."

History is undecided about Custer, as are most writers who have dealt with his character since changing mores brought his heroism into question. Like Henry, Berger presents him as both great soldier and shrieking martinet, but at the moment of truth the latter author steps beyond Henry's interpretation of the commander's literal last laugh—which according to some Indian accounts may be correct—to suggest raving insanity. Berger's picture of Custer prancing, singing, and quoting at length from his own tracts on the nature of the red man while bullets and arrows whiz past epitomizes the razor-edged satire for which the author is known. Irony is his aim, and in this world of Contrary Men and mincing *heemanehs,* of dandified killers and painted whores, of preening jingoists on both sides of the war for the territories, he finds an ideal target.

The Court-Martial of George Armstrong Custer (1976)

Custer as madman also intrigues Douglas C. Jones, whose *Court-Martial of George Armstrong Custer* hangs its hat on the premise that "the white longhair" survived the Little Big Horn to answer charges of gross misconduct before a military tribunal. From this preposterous clay Jones sculpts a stark and believable bas-relief of human lives sacrificed to one man's ambition and arrogance. The effect is nightmarish:

> Then the bugle starts. It is only a short distance down the ridge. The sound is clear and carries well over the rolling swell of ground. A brass bugle. Bought in some Indian trader's store or given as a present to a naked, paint-daubed Plainsman. There is no recognized call, only notes blown at random. It comes closer, then stops abruptly. Sleep begins to creep in, forcing heavy eyelids down. The bugle blasts again, so close the air can be heard rushing through the tubing. It creates fear. Fear of the darkness and what it hides. Again the bugle and someone screams aloud. . . .

If *Court-Martial* has a hero it is Major Asa B. Gardiner,

the trial judge advocate prosecuting Custer. He squares off with wily, club-footed civilian defense counsel Allan Jacobson in a gray area lit intermittently by walk-ons by such luminaries as President Ulysses S. Grant and General William Tecumseh Sherman, while witnesses ranging from Major Marcus Reno and Captain Frederick Benteen to the Crow scout Curly present evidence for and against the commander in the dock. The charged courtroom atmosphere enables Jones to re-create the battle accurately without resorting to Berger's wild speculation or diluting the drama with Henry's exhaustive footnotes.

Jones is clear on the subject of Custer, whose record of insubordination and desertion is used to underscore the impetuous vainglory of his character, and he reserves fiendish punishment for the blunder, forcing him to relive over and over in his fevered mind the horror of his final battle, damning him to an eternity atop Custer Hill. In this manner he renders poignant the sardonic twist at the end of this most controlled and comprehensive fictional account of that popular disaster.

Frontier fiction has known no finer artist than Douglas C. Jones. Although his Sioux trilogy that begins with *Court-Martial* and reaches high flame with *Arrest Sitting Bull* fizzles out in the uninspired centerlessness of *A Creek Called Wounded Knee,* he never loses sight of the greatness of his subject or of the humanity of his characters and remains the only white author who can write consistently and convincingly from an Indian's point of view.

6.

The People

The Searchers (1954)

Where the thread of race winds through literature, emotion follows, distorting the pattern for better or worse socially, almost always for worse historically and artistically. The martyrs who inhabit the Indian villages of much post-sixties-revolution western fiction bear no closer resemblance to the supreme realists of the plains than did the leering savages of the early dime novels. The writer who chooses to approach the red-white conflict objectively, without flinching, had better write well enough to overcome the inevitable outcry from among the descendants of both sides. Alan LeMay writes more than well enough.

A book whose simplicity of plot masks a tangle of unspoken motives and rationales that are anything but simple, *The Searchers* traces the six-year odyssey of two very different men in search of a young girl kidnapped by Comanches across a hostile Southwest as alien as a moonscape. Young, sensitive Martin Pauley, thrown together in the quest with sullen, sixtyish Amos Edwards, wrestles throughout with his partner's monolithic resolve to avenge the murder of his brother and sister-in-law, the frustrations of attempting to follow a dead trail through the shifting alliances and name-changes of this most loosely organized and deadliest of tribes,

71

and, most implacable of all, a nameless, marrow-freezing dread brought on by his own family's massacre, which he witnessed as a child. Psychological trauma, that hoary concept that when forced into a pre-Freudian setting often destroys balance, adds instead a new overlay to LeMay's wickerwork:

> A bitter chill crept along the whole length of his body. The frozen ground seemed to drain the heat from his blood, and the blood from his heart itself. Perhaps it was that, and knowing where he was, that accounted for what happened next. Or maybe scars, almost as old as he was, were still in existence down at the bottom of his mind, long buried under everything that had happened in between. The sky seemed to darken, while a ringing, buzzing sound came into his ears, and when the sky was completely black it began to redden with a bloody glow. His stomach dropped from under his heart, and a horrible fear filled him—the fear of a small helpless child, abandoned and alone in the night. . . .
>
> . . . Then, through a rift in the brush that showed the creek bank, he saw the death tree.
>
> Its base was almost on a level with his eyes, at perhaps a hundred feet; and for one brief moment it seemed to swell and tower, writhing its corpse-withered arms. His eyes stayed fixed upon it as he slowly got up and walked toward it without volition, as if it were the only thing possible to do. The thing shrunk as he approached it, no longer towering over him twice his size . . .
>
> . . . He lashed out and struck it, hard, with the heel of his right hand. The long-rotted roots broke beneath the surface of the soil; and a twisted old stump tottered, splashed in the creek, and went spinning away.
>
> Mart shuddered, shaking himself back together; and he spoke aloud. "I'll be a son-of-a-bitch," he said . . .

But not all of Mart's demons are dispelled with a blow, as he and Amos follow one smoky lead after another throughout the windswept vastness of Texas and New Mexico, Mart driven by guilt and grief for his adopted sister's plight, Amos by hidden inner fires that seem to have burned off his humanity and left only blind hollow hate. He is as much an empty equation as the enigmatic Comanches, and is therefore as dangerous to the success of their mission. There can be no friendship between these two, bound together by necessity. They drift in and out of various Comanche camps, acquiring the language and those customs that will make their search easier, from the outside becoming nearly indistinguishable from the people with whom they are dealing. But only from the outside, as the young Comanche woman Mart takes as a squaw in the belief he is bargaining for her fur learns after only a few days, at the end of which she deserts him for her people. Amos and Mart go out and return home and go out again, staying away longer each time until the search itself becomes home, and home only a place to secure fresh mounts. The woman Mart might have married loses patience and weds another. Having run afoul of the Texas Rangers, the searchers grow wary of their own kind. It has become easier to stay out than to go back.

The Comaches are as merciless as the land they inhabit. To them a white woman is something to be used and then destroyed, her severed arm to be tossed playfully from buck to buck until they tire of the game and ride away. They murder the white man's male offspring lest they sire more of their hated race, take along his small girls that they may grow up Comanche. LeMay turns his back on the aching sentimentality of the losing of the West, avoiding sympathy by setting his story in a time when the Indians reigned unchallenged:

> More often you had to remember landmarks to locate where a place had been at all. Generally your horse stumbled over an old footing or something before you saw the flat place

where the little houses had been. Sometimes you found graves here, too, but more usually the people had simply pulled their house down and hauled the lumber away, retreating from a place the Peace Policy had let become too deadly, coming on top of the war. You got the impression that Texas had seen its high tide, becoming little again as its frontier thinned away. . . .

Bigoted writers aware of their bigotry expose that awareness by casting their stories with opposites; for every band of brutal Indians they provide a noble brave, hoping thereby to forestall criticism. But there are no noble savages in *The Searchers,* only men and women on both sides hardened by the awful burden of survival into unthinking cruelty. Amos Edwards' silence, admirable in Shane and the Virginian, is here as sinister as a diamondback without rattles. In him, LeMay reflects those same stresses that have given the Comanches their bitter edge. It is one of the book's many ironies that Edwards' tragic fate springs not from the stony bank he has erected as protection against the harsh realities of his time and place, but from the barely glowing spark of humanity he has sought to protect.

Mart's existence beyond the tale's quietly heart-stopping conclusion is difficult to envision. The Comanches' twilight is at hand, and with it that of the fevered, driving way of life Mart has led for so long. His search is ended, the girl rescued, but there is nothing for them to go back to. In every way this hero has come to embody the smoky name the Indians have given him: The Other.

Hombre (1961)

Amos Edwards and John Russell, the title character of Elmore Leonard's *Hombre,* would understand each other.

A white man raised by Apaches, Russell boards the last stage out of Sweetmary, Arizona, bound for civilization and a new and unfamiliar life among others of his race. But trouble follows him as it followed Shane, and he finds himself guarding twelve thousand dollars in stolen government funds meant for an Apache reservation and a dwindling water supply from a gang of ruthless desperadoes. Like LeMay, Leonard trades cold blood for cold blood, balancing the sides, Russell's indifference to human suffering against the Mexican's gleeful sadism and Frank Braden's murderous greed. The hero's Sphinx-like demeanor upsets and confuses those passengers depending on him for survival afoot in the desert, including Carl Allen, a tenderfoot narrator who like *The Virginian*'s storyteller looks upon the adversaries as upon a foreign breed:

> "What's the difference who has the money?" the Mexican said. "You give it to us or we shoot that woman."
>
> "All right," Russell said. "You shoot her."
>
> The Mexican kept staring at him. "What about the rest of them? What do they say?"
>
> "They say what they want," Russell said. "I say what I want. Do you see that now?"
>
> He didn't see it. He didn't know what to think, so he just stood there, one hand at his side, the other holding that truce flag.
>
> "Tell Braden how it is," Russell said. "Tell him to think some more." . . .
>
> The Mexican hadn't taken his eyes off Russell for a second, sizing him up all the while they talked. "Maybe you and I finish something first," he said. "Maybe you come down here a little."
>
> "I'm thinking," Russell said, "whether to kill you right now or wait till you turn around."
>
> Do you know what the Mexican did? He smiled. Not that unbelieving kind of smile, but like he appreciated Russell or enjoyed him. It was about the strangest thing I ever saw. . . .

In an arena of sun and sand, only professional gladiators understand each other.

Leonard's stark method, nude of images and introspection and fueled by brittle dialogue, is well suited to his choice of setting. Like LeMay's Texas, Arizona's hostile terrain hardly invites the finer points of civilization or of literary pretension. His prose has the raw vitality of something dashed off in a marathon fever of inspiration, but by its very simplicity indicating the thousand stresses beneath the surface. It is as visual as a filmscript and as immediate as an exchange of gunfire in the desert.

Growth is of little importance to the central figure in this novel, whose pace and cohesion most closely resemble the strengths of a Hemingway short story. The characters of the crooked Indian agent, his wife, the girl recently rescued from the Apaches, the Mexican who runs the stage station, and narrator Allen become vivid as the various stresses peel away their careful veneers, but from opening to climax Russell remains the same, because there was no veneer there to begin with. (The Apache upbringing that seems gratuitous in L'Amour's Hondo and of little importance to his adventure bears constantly on Leonard's hero.) So too with Frank Braden, which is Leonard's message. The two were destined to tangle, for they are too much alike. And because they are alike, any confrontation between them must end in stalemate. At this point Leonard falls back on a LeMay tactic, allowing a fissure of fellow human feeling to appear in Russell's dam of indifference and the tensions that have been building since the first page to burst through. Russell meets his end not at Braden's hands but at those of civilization (although for Braden the victory is Pyrrhic). This is as apt a comment on the death of the West as has ever been made in microcosm.

Arrest Sitting Bull (1977)

"I do not think my spirit is ready yet to become a white man," declares Standing Elk, the fictional hero of Douglas

C. Jones's largely historical *Arrest Sitting Bull,* and so identifies the spark that touches off the powder in this thoughtful
and moving study of a vanquished race struggling to enter
the world of its conquerors.

The year is 1890, the place the Sioux reservation at Standing Rock, South Dakota, where the remnants of the vengeful
horde that swept over the Seventh Cavalry in Jones's *Court-
Martial of George Armstrong Custer* are now chewing the
bitter cud of defeat. Some, like Chief Gall, accept their new
role with what dignity is left them; others, most prominently
Sitting Bull himself, embrace a bastard creed born in desperation of ancient tribal ritual and the white man's promise
of a Second Coming. Still others, like young Standing Elk,
caught between the road traveled by their ancestors and the
one white society has prepared for them, choose counterfeit
warriorship among the ranks of the reservation police.

The story does not lack for troubled heroes. Perhaps the
most besieged is James McLaughlin, the Indian agent in
charge of Standing Rock, who battles to maintain peace between his red wards and a paranoiac Washington bureaucracy
determined to squash by any means an imagined revolt in
Sitting Bull's Ghost Dance hysteria. And there is a splendidly
burlesque cameo played by William Frederick "Buffalo Bill"
Cody, sent by General Nelson A. Miles to take Sitting Bull
into custody with a small band of armed men and a wagonload of hard candy.

When an attempt by McLaughlin and his ally, Lieutenant
Colonel William Drum, to drink the bibulous Cody under
the table and thus prevent the expedition fails gloriously, the
conspirators resort to guile and misdirect the arresting party
until a wire to President Harrison can effect a withdrawal of
Miles's order. It is the one light moment in a tragedy whose
end is obvious to those with foresight, particularly Sitting
Bull:

But if the Old Bull has fooled most white men and many
of his own people as well, he has not fooled himself. He is
a man trying to recapture enough of the old spirit to show
the white man how a proud people die.

Running counterpoint to the grand tragedy is the small
poignancy of Willa Mae Favory, a teacher at the mission
school threatened by approaching spinsterhood, and of her
love for Standing Elk. Shyly the couple tiptoes around the
courtship ritual, made thornier by its forbidden nature between members of alien cultures, but the gravity of their
mutual attraction is slowly gaining ground when dark Fate
intervenes. She will be an old maid and her lover will be
buried in full Sioux state, a casualty, along with Sitting Bull
himself, of a badly mismanaged effort by the reservation
police to arrest the old medicine man.

A suffocating inexorability reminiscent of *The Ox-Bow
Incident* overhangs this story of men and women rushing to
forestall events already ordained. The end is as inevitable as
the elements:

> Winter comes at last, sending the cold winds from the north
> blowing hard across the desolate Dakota plains east of the
> Missouri, pushing the last dried husks of prairie grass across
> the land. In the sudden gusts crows are swept along, soaring
> without effort, wings like black shingles motionless against
> the gray, scudding clouds. Their cries are whipped out thin
> and brittle in the strong currents, and the hunting call of the
> red tail is lost completely. Along the stream beds the rabbit
> ice thrusts up like quartz crystal, popping underfoot. The old
> ones say the snow is not far away now.

The stage is set for the melancholy horror of Wounded
Knee, and of the Carthaginian destruction of a proud race.

Few writers can match the eloquence of Jones's empathy for the unquestionably doomed. If *The Sea of Grass* and *Monte Walsh* are ballads of lost days, *Arrest Sitting Bull* is a ringing chant of death.

7.

Mile High

The Big Sky (1952)

Paradise is a favorite theme of epic western novelists. Wister ends *The Virginian* on an untrammeled island in the mountains, where the hero and his bride spend their honeymoon. Zane Grey's Venters, and eventually Lassiter and Jane Withersteen, find peace against the breathtaking backdrop of Surprise Valley. Shane's idyll with the Starretts, and Clayton's years with the Sioux, are pastoral retreats from their lives of violence. The pull of the return to innocence is basic and stronger than gravity.

In *The Big Sky*, A. B. Guthrie, Jr.'s towering saga of mountain men in the early Northwest, the strain of the fall from grace finds a true refrain. Driven into the wilderness by the cruelty of his father and the inspiration of his impressive frontiersman uncle, Boone Caudill carves a primitive life out of the mountainscape with friend Jim Deakins. Over this sparse Old Testament framework Guthrie stretches an episodic tapestry of virgin beauty woven from his intimate knowledge of and love for the frontier. The colors are hypnotic:

> The country climbed and fell and rolled away in such great sweeps that a man sometimes felt small as any ant. It was a country of stone and timber and quick, clear creeks and the Gallatin rushing through it, turning and twisting, and the

noise of it beating steady against the ears. Lower down, the river slid into the mixed waters of the Madison and Jefferson, making the Missouri sure enough. Here was the heart of Blackfoot land, the Three Forks, where many a hunter had died, where even big parties didn't like to go, knowing war parties would be after them thick and fierce as hornets; but there were no Indians about them now, only signs of them, only cold campfires and gnawed bones where villages had stood and old clumps of sod the squaws had dug to hold the lodge skins down. . . .

Into this dangerous Eden comes Eve, a Blackfoot girl named Teal Eye, whom Caudill takes as his squaw. They know euphoria until the birth of their blind child, and then the serpent glides in in the person of an Indian named Bear to play Iago to the mountaineer's Othello. Caudill then plays Cain and is cast out. "You no come back," Teal Eye tells him. Dying by his friend's jealous hand, Jim remarks: "I'll know about God, I reckon, now."

Paradise violated cannot stand, and in a foreshadowing of Vardis Fisher's tic-like obsession with the Mormon crawl in *Mountain Man,* a disgraced Caudill discusses with fellow pioneer Dick Summers the ramifications of the coming Oregon land rush, leaving unspoken the knowledge that their way of life is ending. But for Caudill it is already over. "Goo'bye," one friend wishes him. "Goo'bye, sad man."

Biblical parallels, here and in the *Exodus*-inspired *Way West,* are a Guthrie trademark, and oddly appropriate to his grand vision. From the blue ice peaks of the Grand Tetons to the howling crystal torrent of the Seedskeedee, through the hunting grounds of the Blackfeet, Ute, and Arikara, across the Snake and the Cheyenne, Guthrie blazes a trail that few writers dare follow, and that all who do must acknowledge. Like Fisher and Gordon D. Shirreffs and Bill Hotchkiss after him, he inlays his pages with giddy mountain air and sharp woodsmoke and profanes Zane Grey's fairy-tale frontier with the blood and manure of horses and men. Grey and Jack Schaefer (in *Shane*) write about the West that should have been. Guthrie, with some liberal borrowing from Holy Writ, writes about the West that likely was.

Mountain Man (1965)

At a casual glance, Vardis Fisher's *Mountain Man* owes more to Ned Buntline than either Owen Wister or Guthrie. For in the eyes of Sam Minard, Fisher's titular hero, the so-called red lords of the mountains and the plains are bug-eating savages who roll their eyes and spit in the faces of tortured white captives and generally behave as the one-dimensional cutouts who raped and massacred their way through the pages of *Beadle's Dime Library* a century ago.

Although Minard, himself a well-rounded individual whose education and technical knowledge of classical music seem at sea in his gigantic frame, has trained himself to distinguish between the scents of the various high country tribes, he notes little fundamental difference among them; and when evidence found at the scene of the murders of his Indian wife Lotus and their infant son points to the supposedly friendly Crows, he asks no questions, but declares war on the entire nation. For readers, this may be a salubrious turn in his character.

For until that point, Minard cuts an archly ludicrous silhouette against the northwestern mountainscape, waving his great arms exaggeratedly like some cartoon maestro while riding naked through a tempest, or soliloquizing at tiresome length on the lack of taxes and tariffs in the wilderness. Despite some small stirrings of regard for the silent and pensive Lotus, who is still awaiting a third dimension when tragedy strikes, one almost welcomes her demise against the prospect of a family of insufferably smug Minards coupling and multiplying in the primordial peace.

The incident galvanizes the mountain man and rescues the book from a morass of undigested historical anecdotes and cooking recipes. Fully expecting to die in his quest for vengeance, Minard says his good-byes to a coterie of smoke-darkened characters ranging from the historical Jim Bridger to the fictional Kate, left crazed and alone after the massacre of her husband and children by the Blackfeet and later offhandedly disposed of by Fisher once she has served her purpose, and proceeds to carve his legend out of granite cliffs stained with the blood of the braves he has slain. As it grows, so does he, notwithstanding an occasional relapse, as when he waxes maudlin over the fate of a young warrior who has just failed in an attempt to strangle Minard to death in a river. The first time he displays any affection for the red race, in fact, occurs after he swears eternal enmity, and it flares up again at predictable intervals until the story fizzles out in a clumsy and anachronistic projection of a twentieth-century wilderness corrupted by cities and people.

The book's strength lies in its close attention to period detail and the brooding sense of doom that overshadows Minard's paradise:

> How will I die? Sam wondered, and sniffed the night air for scent of Blackfeet. How would Lotus die? He was sure that neither of them would die in bed. Few whitemen in this land had sense enough, when eyes and trigger finger began to fail, to pack their possibles and get out. . . .

There are some impressive touches. Minard's grueling trek following his escape from the Blackfeet wins him a place in mountain lore. The mad widow Kate repays her debt to him with a warm berth at the end of his journey. He and the Crow chief, weary of bloodshed at last, smoke the pipe of peace so that they may return to their traditional ways. Rude honor is the coin of this realm. If Fisher suffers from an excess of narrative digressions and a jerkily episodic structure, his readers benefit from a closer understanding of the hermits who braved sudden country. Plainly, he loves his subject, and while he may overreach he does not shrink back, and for all its flaws, *Mountain Man* remains a landmark along the Wister Trace.

The Untamed Breed (1981)

Gordon D. Shirreffs, by 1981 a three-decade veteran of western prose and a contemporary of Guthrie's at the time the latter was doing his best work, can hardly be termed a chronological successor, and yet he is the only artist working steadily today who combines Guthrie's poetic flare with an intimate personal knowledge of the frontier. *The Untamed Breed* takes the reader from the dramatic verticals Boone Caudill and Dick Summers knew to the mesquite-carpeted flats of New Mexico and the Great Southwest, which is Shirreffs' chief interest and first love. Grand settings require characters to compare with them, and the author obliges:

> Quintin Ker-Shaw, Scots-Canadian known to men as Quint Kershaw and to mountain men as Big Red . . . was a veritable panther of a man, six feet two inches tall, 190 pounds of lean, sinewy muscle and bone. He was hawk-eyed and hawk-nosed and had a thick and greasy sorrel beard. His fine even teeth were pure white in contrast to the saddle-brown hue of his weathered countenance. His reddish hair had been woven into two thick braids, wrapped in shining otter skin and hung in front of his broad shoulders. A small silver ring shone in his left earlobe. His hat was a shapeless, battered creation of rough wool with a rattlesnake-skin band

into which had been stuck a gray eagle feather. He wore a heavy, scantily beaded mid-thigh-length elkskin jacket over a thick woolen shirt. His wrinkled seatless full-length buckskin leggins were fringed with Blackfoot hair. His loincloth was of thick red flannel. The clothing was glazed and smutted with grease, dirt, ashes, dried animal blood, sweat and dribbled whiskey; a frosty look of absolute filth . . .

Shirreffs' subtle use of language distinguishes between "men" and "mountain men," establishing Kershaw's breed as a race apart. His is a world in which "a frosty look of absolute filth" is a symbol of stature acquired during a season's honest trapping and skinning. Cleanliness is suspect in this subculture, first defined as such by Owen Wister.

If Caudill's humorlessness is his fatal flaw, Kershaw doesn't share it. Danger and hardship have thrust a black wit upon him that is both his distinction and his armor:

Quint approached the head on the stump. He bent a little and looked closely at it despite his revulsion. It *looked* like Jim Slocum. Quint figured from the scattered body parts that there must have been three or four men in the party.

. . . He tipped his hat as he passed the head on the stump. "Don't bother tae get up, Mr. Slocum," he murmured politely in his clipped Scots.

One can imagine Sam Minard claiming the same opportunity to decry for a page and a half the red man's congenital brutality, finishing in tasty instructions on how to prepare roast head of bighorn sheep.

With his partners Luke Connors, François Charbonne, and Moccasin, a Delaware brave, Kershaw patrols a paradise hardly recognizable as such for the presence of marauding Comancheros, the political intrigues leading up to the Mexican War, and the creeping white man's death of smallpox. Like Caudill and Minard he finds his Eve among the savages

and fathers a son; like Minard he loses his woman to hostiles.
He knows a guilt similar to Caudill's for having succumbed
to the wilderness call when he was needed in his lodge. In
a reverse twist on *Riders of the Purple Sage,* his misfortunes
begin upon discovering a beautiful hidden valley, culminat-
ing in a deadly knife duel with the Comanchero Antonio,
a villain whose smiling evil echoes Trampas and Stark Wilson
and the anonymous bandits in B. Traven's *Treasure of the
Sierra Madre.* Paradise cannot abide on earth, only a treacherous substitute. "Its pleasantness," notes Shirreffs' narration, "was a deception; a perilous Eden."

Uncompromising in detail, *The Untamed Breed* and its
immediate sequels, *Bold Legend* and *Glorieta Pass,* may
prove slow going for the casual reader accustomed to
stampeding hoofs and staccato bursts of gunfire on hardpack
streets. But the integrity of these first volumes in a proposed
saga of the early Southwest from the Alamo through the
Civil War lies in the author's ability to balance the crisis of
the individual with the long sure roll of history.

The Medicine Calf (1981)

Given as gospel the test of time as the guideline, the "in-
stant classic" is an impossibility. Yet *The Medicine Calf,* Bill
Hotchkiss' smoothly paced novelization of nine years in the
life of mountain-man-turned-Crow-chief Jim Beckwourth,
has all the earmarks of that hybrid beloved of editors who
write publicity blurbs.

Hotchkiss has chosen his subject wisely, for the milieu of
an alien society unfolds most naturally when both hero and
reader are encountering it for the first time, as did John Clayton in *No Survivors* and Jack Crabb in *Little Big Man;* the
alternative, that of an Indian explaining his own customs and

traditions, makes one wonder why he is telling of these things that everyone is supposed to know—a mistake Will Henry himself makes in *From Where the Sun Now Stands,* a book often regarded as his masterpiece. But Hotchkiss' third person is less pedantic than the subjective voice of either Clayton or Crabb:

> The village of Long Hair arrived at the Rose Bud, and the people, together, entered into a period of general mourning. Long Hair cut off a large roll of his hair, and the Crows knew that the great chief had never done such a thing before. More fingers were lopped off, and many braves, after the example of Long Hair, also cut off portions of their hair. Some of the warriors cut twin gashes the length of their arms and then, having separated the skin from the flesh at one end, would grasp the hide with the other hand and rip it back to the shoulder. Some cut designs upon breast or shoulder and lifted the skin in a similar manner, thus producing, when the wounds healed, highly visible scars.

This straightforward setting-down of extraordinary facts examines a singular mode of life without ridiculing those who follow it.

A professional poet, Hotchkiss nonetheless avoids Guthrie's lyricism except in italicized epigraphs to his chapters, keeping his story moving with spare language and brittle dialogue. But the earth growls as loudly beneath the tread of buffalo, and the blood of the slain runs as quick and bright for what he has left unsaid. What results is that rare equation, an epic told with economy and restraint.

Epic it is, as the narrative follows the progress of a black slave who rises to the highest level a Crow warrior can attain. But the Horatio Alger angle plays gentle counterpoint to Hotchkiss's tale of cultures in conflict.

Of the handful of western novels that have attained landmark status, even fewer are based on the lives of historical figures. The writer who has chosen to work in a highly specialized field narrows his options further by inviting the tyranny of the real. Often he but retells things already known; oftener still he romanticizes them beyond recognition and would as well have begun with a fictional concept altogether. Bill Hotchkiss does neither, electing instead to cloak the lean bones of Jim Beckwourth's own memoirs in the flesh of personal experience and close research. Just what his place will be in the scheme of frontier writers who have reflected credit on their art may depend on his future work, but *The Medicine Calf* guarantees him a place.

8.

Hot Irons

Just because their role in the multiple-act passion play of the West was small doesn't mean they didn't exist. Yet there are fundamentalists who would rewrite the history of American western literature to exclude all references to professional gunmen and forge ahead with tales of placid wagon trains and Nebraska farmers who lived and died in their furrows and never saw a muzzle flash. Three of our best contemporary storytellers have refused to comply with this dictum and, taking authenticity as their watchword, have delivered a trio of modern classics about the men who first captured readers' hearts in New York and Chicago and never knew they were performing in a mere sideshow to the center ring.

True Grit (1968)

Due in part to its dime-novel title and the broad but effective portrayal of Rooster Cogburn by John Wayne in the motion picture, *True Grit* is often dismissed as an affectionate satire of the border tales of the nineteenth century. Instead, it is an accurate and highly entertaining treatment of late Victorian morality cast adrift in that motley sea of hardship and shocking depravity known as the Nations in what is now Oklahoma, and goes beyond Owen Wister's view of the West as an alien world to suggest that its heroes were very much a part of that world.

No honest and taciturn Virginian is Marshal Cogburn; drunkard and braggart, he kills for the sake of convenience and sells his victims' horses and tack to line his pockets. Young heroine Mattie Ross' first impressions scarcely resemble Jack Schaefer's boy-narrator's initial introduction to Shane:

> I had guessed wrong as to which one he was, picking out a younger and slighter man with a badge on his shirt, and I was surprised when an old one-eyed jasper that was built along the lines of Grover Cleveland went up and was sworn. I say "old." He was about forty years of age. The floor boards squeaked under his weight. He was wearing a dusty black suit of clothes and when he sat down I saw that his badge was on his vest. It was a little silver circle with a star in it. He had a moustache like Cleveland too.

Cogburn's appearance and character closely follow existing profiles of the deputy marshals who rode for "Hanging Judge" Isaac Parker in the Nations.

Counterbalancing his unkempt garrulity, much as Venters' civilized veneer complements the coiled danger of Lassiter, is Jules LaBoeuf, an arrogant young Texas Ranger eager to collect the reward offered for the arrest of Tom Chaney, the man who killed Mattie's father. The pair's mutual distrust leads to sparkling exchanges of dialogue, which author Charles Portis couches coyly in the archaic phraseology of the McGuffey era. They lug this schoolhouse baggage into a raw country where families are slaughtered for a few dollars buried in the backyard and would-be informants' fingers fly up "like chips of wood" when severed by knife-swinging badmen. Portis' choice of formal English in a savage setting lends the sure tone of period to the dramatic climax, when Cogburn sheds his clown make-up to reveal the Virginian beneath:

Lucky Ned Pepper said, "What is your intention? Do you think one on four is a dogfall?"

Rooster said, "I mean to kill you in one minute, Ned, or see you hanged in Fort Smith at Judge Parker's convenience! Which will you have?"

Lucky Ned Pepper laughed. He said, "I call that bold talk for a one-eyed fat man!"

Rooster said, "Fill your hand, you son of a bitch!"

Combining colorful action with period detail and an unshakable faith in the meanest man's nobility, *True Grit* is a good-humored tall tale told with the adolescent energy of Buffalo Bill's Wild West in performance. Few writers approach Charles Portis' assured knowledge and love of subject. To read him is to leave behind the gray Kansas reaches and look out on Oz.

Wild Times (1978)

Wild Times is the dime novel that *True Grit* has been accused of being, and that is author Brian Garfield's intention. Here he uncorks a storyteller's sense gained from a youth spent in the West and the knowledge acquired from a lifetime of research to spin a yarn of giants against buckskin-colored plains and bright steel skies.

Six-foot-five-inch Colonel Hugh Cardiff—sharpshooter, scout, and showman, loosely structured on Buffalo Bill—sheds bullets like perspiration and crosses shadows with the like of Wild Bill Hickok and Doc Holliday in a West best described as a distillation from the writings of Francis Parkman and Ned Buntline. In fact, Buntline makes an appearance in the guise of Bob Halburton, an alcoholic itinerant temperance lecturer and writer of popular fiction whose thrillers with Cardiff as hero catapult the adventurer to national fame.

In a refreshing throwback to *The Virginian* and *Riders of the Purple Sage,* the pursuit of the heroine—in this case Libby Tyree—becomes a major theme and the motive for many of the hero's actions. Around this spindle, stiffened by the near-psychotic enmity of Libby's Trampas-like brother Vernon, Garfield winds a string of astonishing length and flexibility, encompassing the physical and moral impedimenta of late Victorian America from Long Island to the Pacific and below the border in revolutionary Mexico (and Europe, although a substantial episode in the Franco-Prussian War was arbitrarily eliminated in editing), as Cardiff goes from tenderfoot kid to old campaigner gambling his fortune and his pride on his fading marksmanship:

> Vern and I had practiced and exercised and trained with grueling dedication for the tournament but I suppose other men had as well. We knew what we were about, he and I; that was what it came down to at the end when we were the only contestants left on that empty smoke-stinking field. What we lacked in youth we made up for in the canny ability to conserve ourselves. Doc Bogardus had taught me every economy of effort. All I had to do was hold the rifle up throughout the fifteen-shot magazine run.
>
> But dear sweet Jesus it was getting hard to hold it up.

The surprise, when it comes, flies straight out of left field, a Garfield trademark.

His irreverent treatment of frontier icons and shrewd eye for human failings reflect a fine sense of the satiric that in Thomas Berger sometimes threatens to overwhelm the story, but that in Garfield is very much a part of that story. Have fun with history, he counsels, but don't trust it. Says Cardiff: "I mean to set down an account of it as straight as I can but you have to keep in mind that I used to have something of a reputation as a liar."

Desperadoes (1979)

Since America's Caesarean birth in the throes of revolution, the theme of the man outside the law has been dominant in its native fiction. Americans are fascinated by bandits. *Desperadoes* represents author Ron Hansen's attempt to deromanticize the Robin Hood myth by portraying the Dalton gang as little more than high-spirited youngsters and by exposing the hardships of life on the scout.

A late entry in the increasingly popular trend toward "frame" westerns, the book opens with an aging Emmett Dalton, last surviving member of the gang, in Hollywood during the Depression helping prepare a film treatment of those violent days. Like all old men he spends most of his time reminiscing as an escape from his stultifying marriage to an old woman who loved him when he was young and wanted, and from a multitude of aches and pains that can no longer be attributed to his bullet scars. The story walks a tightrope between the chiaroscuro of decades and pungent reality, mingling fleeting, heroic images of tall men in new Stetsons and floor-length dusters brandishing big Colts, with boring bathless weeks in the saddle and frostbitten fingers and toes waiting for the next train to rob.

Their drift into outlawry is almost a natural evolution from their appointment to Hanging Judge Isaac Parker's court, where as peace officers maintaining order in the wild Indian Nations they succumb to the constant opportunities for graft and corruption and fall to rustling horses and selling whiskey to the Indian settlers. From there it is a short hop to robbing trains:

> . . . I saw Newcomb masked and on his horse with the
> sleeves rolled up on his raincoat, his rifle barrel propped on
> the open platform between the express and baggage cars. I

walked my horse along mostly dark passenger cars and to the empty caboose. In order to demonstrate to God and man what a young tough I was, I broke the glass tail lamp with the butt of my pistol and flame tore away from the wick. When I bent I could see the legs of Pierce's and Broadwell's horses. I saw a man walk out on a center coach platform lighting a cigarette. I raised my rifle high over my head and nodded at Newcomb and both of us fired warning shots, as did Broadwell and Pierce, so that it sounded like iron doors banging shut in a house of many rooms. . . . There were yells and screams about holdups and the train being robbed. The lights went out in all the cars. Faces disappeared from the windows. Steam leaked out from under the wheels.

Hansen's photographic eye is what gives *Desperadoes* its unique stamp. Where a broken lamp is as important as the noise of gunfire, the picture that emerges is as authentic as a Brady print. Horses prance and bob their heads and snort milky vapor; locomotives are "black and hot and big as a shoe store." It is the poetry of the everyday.

The heroes, Emmett and Bob and Grat Dalton and the men who ride with them, are all young enough to enjoy their notoriety, and even a mature character like Eugenia Moore, the schoolteacher who takes up with leader Bob, cannot stay away from the intoxicating aura of doom that surrounds them, although she tries. They are doomed not so much because of their illegal ways as because the world is turning away from them toward civilization, and in the turning crushes them. That action carries a supreme indifference. Even their last fateful raid is captured by an early motion-picture camera "on film that is now orange and disintegrating," like any moderately interesting event staged for the entertainment of the mildly curious. Afterward a fly crawls inside Bob Dalton's dead mouth.

In the end it is not a romance at all, but a show. The friends and neighbors of the Daltons who shot them to pieces on that autumn day in 1892 slink forward to smile and grasp Emmett's hand in 1937. Adversaries no longer, they are fellow survivors of a forgotten reality.

9.

Greed and Gods

The Treasure of the Sierra Madre (1935)

In his Howard Hughes-like obsession with privacy, the mysterious "B. Traven" behind *The Treasure of the Sierra Madre* has drawn more critical attention than his fevered tale of greed and murder told against a Mexican mountainscape. Speculation concerning the author's actual identity has included Jack London and Ambrose Bierce, and despite Will Wyatt's exhaustive and convincing argument in favor of a German national named Otto Wienecke in his 1980 study, *The Secret of the Sierra Madre*, the game will likely continue. No one loves a good mystery like a literarian.

This bibliophilic foxhunt has tended to obscure the value of Traven's book as a patient scrutiny of civilized man reverting to savage. In this it is more riveting and believable than Nobel laureate William Golding's moralistic allegorical treatment of the same theme in *Lord of the Flies*.

Three men hurled together by fate and their empty bellies leave behind the twentieth-century oilfields to seek a fortune in gold in the primitive Sierras south of the border. Strangers, they never become friends, calling one another by surnames only, their partnership based solely on mutual need. The lion's share of the stake is put up by Dobbs, whose lottery windfall will in time bear grim resemblance to that in Shirley Jackson's classic short story.

The "Treasure" of the title is sardonic. No rainbow cache of easy wealth this, but drab dust chipped out of solid rock with pickaxes under a white sun nailed to a bronze sky. So the long days and weeks and months—longer yet by general agreement—chip away at the trio's humanity. Howard alone, an old and benevolent Lord Henry to Dobbs and Curtin's Dorian Gray, outwardly retains his Christianity, but as he discusses the problem of a meddlesome fourth party, his role as a fiendishly subtle Iago is arguable:

> ". . . We might tell him that we've committed a couple of murders and are hiding out. But suppose he's the wrong kind; he'll go back after a while and set a company of federal troops after us. If they get you, and the officer in command is in a hurry to return to his jane, he orders his soldiers to shoot you like a sick dog. They shoot you while you are trying to escape. You can't prove afterwards that they were mistaken, because they bury you right where you drop, and before that they make you dig a hole to spend your time in until the trumpets call you to check up the register of your sins."

"Then there's nothing left to do but pull the trigger the very minute he comes," suggests Dobbs.

Assuredly, their environment does not invite trust. The authorities are xenophobes, the mountains crawl with bandits and hostile Indians, and even the odd gentle villager may carry away a story that will bring all of these elements down on the prospectors. Everything that grows has either spines or fangs.

Traven's writing suffers from occasional self-consciousness, and his difficulty with natural dialogue and apparent unfamiliarity with American slang present a compelling case for Will Wyatt's conclusion that the author was foreign-born. Yet his understanding of basic human emotions transcends language.

It's a short step from plotting a stranger's murder to killing one's own partners, and as distrust grows along with each man's share of the gold, Dobbs takes it, shooting Curtin and leaving him for dead. With Howard's help Curtin survives, and the hunt begins. But there are other hunters at large:

> "Oiga, señor, listen. We are no bandits. You are mistaken. We are the policía montada, the mounted police, you know. We are looking for the bandits, to catch them. They have robbed the train, you know."
>
> "All right," Curtin shouted back. "If you are the police, where are your badges? Let's see them."
>
> "Badges, to goddamned hell with badges! . . ."

It is a country of mirages, where bandits masquerade as men of law, hungry animals as friends, and gold as common dirt to be scattered by the wind even as Dobbs's neck is still pumping blood, his head taken by human scavengers out to sell his burros and hides for money to eat. Wealth is relative and illusory. Of the surviving partners, only Howard is capable of appreciating this, and of stating Traven's truth: "I think it is a very good joke."

Under the Fifth Sun (1980)

The Mexican bandit trades his stereotyped grinning perfidy for the stuff of myth in *Under the Fifth Sun,* Earl Shorris' multiple-level epic ode to revolution and the enigma that was Pancho Villa. Often portrayed as an uncouth drunk and brigand, this Villa is a sensitive man of deep moral conviction whose love affair with Cervantes leads him from common outlawry into the rebellion against Porfirio Díaz, and eventually against injustice itself.

On the surface the revenge motif, a western staple, explains young Doroteo Arango's drift into lawlessness after his father's early death in the fields and his sister's rape by the local feudal lord. On another, social level, the rage of generations of serfdom in which men die young and their widows grub on comes to a boil in a youth whose concept of right and wrong is as sharply defined as the caves of Chihuahua, for decades the refuge of bandits, among them that other Pancho Villa, whose name Doroteo assumes in the rebels' traditional denial of identity. But there is yet a third level.

For the story is told by an Aztec shaman, ancient at the time of Doroteo's birth, and who lives to tell of Villa's death, cooking his roots and herbs in the high desert country of Canatlán and making dreams that foretell a future known for centuries and destined to be fulfilled by a peasant lad with one genetic foot in Spain and the other in Indian tribal heritage. These passages twist and coil in the thick, evil-smelling smoke clouding the prophet's mirror:

> Motecuhzoma Xocoyotzin is dead, Cuahtemoc could not save us, the weeping woman of the streets of Mexico City is not an illusion. We are poor people now. We work like ants in a place surrounded by endless seas. Perhaps this is the last world, the final sun. I am merely the smoke that sits in the plaza of San Juan del Rio or Canatlán on Saturday nights. I know nothing but the names of the directions, the thirteen heavens, the nine hells and the One-who-made-himself-of-his-own-thoughts. There is a Place of Mystery called Death, which is the only name that has no face. These are the truths I tell to the children on Saturday nights when they come to the plaza to listen to the music and learn the glances of courtship. These are the things I tell them in the vulnerable moment when they dream that they are not ants.

This is Villa's dream, and he sets out to make it true. As his hero Don Quixote defended the illusive chastity of Dulcinea, so this unwashed knight sheds Mexican federal blood for the rebel President Madero, himself weak and prey to his self-serving advisors. For the crime of popularity he is imprisoned by one of them, General Huerta, he of the tinted glasses and limited vision, and made to crack in front of a firing squad to destroy his support among the citizens and the revolutionary army before he is pardoned. "He felt the dust in his clothes and he thought for the first time of the shame," recalls the omniscient shaman; "he thought for the first time he had not been a man."

But Huerta, who in his ambition for personal power is as naïve as Villa himself in his worship of an unworthy Madero, has not reckoned on the depth of the country's disillusionment, or on the fact that a disgraced hero is preferable to no hero at all. Even a shattering (and probably duplicitous) defeat on the eve of final victory cannot destroy him, any more than can a twentieth-century United States Army bent on vengeance for Villa's infamous raid on Columbus, New Mexico. Desert cactus that he is, he survives, listening to the conversation of the gringo soldiers searching for him outside the cave where he lies wounded and bleeding.

Lusting but not lusty, Shorris' Villa cannot lie with a woman who is not his wife, and so he marries all his prospective mistresses. Calumniated from New York to Mexico City as an unprincipled bandit, he alone, unlike the vacillating and assassination-doomed Madero and the megalomaniacal Huerta and the muddled-Marxist Emilio Zapata, upholds the revolution's youthful ideals. He is as misunderstood as Sam Chance and as chained to his fate as Shane, but he persists, the soul of rebellion. A lost war and his own murder by a new government still fearful of the aging tiger in its midst only underscore this:

> He brought the brigades together, all the brigades from all
> the towns and all the states, the cowboys and the farmers,

the professors and the wanderers, the storekeepers and the soldiers who sought a different army. The trains of his army overflowed the railroad yards, his horses filled the spaces between cities. He was the general of artillery and infantry and cavalry, he was the general of generals; thirty thousand men passed in review before him in a single day. He learned reading and socialism, he loved the poor. He built schools for the children of the revolution, he began the division of the land.

Under the Fifth Sun is a work of emotion and scope, performing Caesarean section on a new century born in blood from the old. While it owes much to techniques pioneered by Gabriel Garcia Marquez, it succeeds in pushing the boundaries of western literature to the very edges of imagination.

The White Buffalo (1975)

The White Buffalo similarly employs spiritualism and romantic realism to tell a smaller story, though one no less poignant. "All of this happened a long time ago," begins Richard Sales, establishing the once-upon-a-time mood of his tale of two seasoned warriors from vastly different cultures thrown together Traven-like in a single obsession, the quest for the fabled albino beast of the title.

A noted gunman is haunted by a recurring nightmare in which a demonic white buffalo charges him across a field of snow. When he reaches down to bring his ubiquitous matched revolvers into play, they aren't there. Convinced that the dream is an omen of his own death, he determines to seek out and destroy the buffalo before the prophecy is fulfilled. Simultaneously, a famed Sioux brave is obsessed with a similar vision that he interprets to mean he must kill the same beast so that his small dead daughter may enter

Sioux paradise and not wander forever in the shadows between worlds. Armed with two views toward the same end,
one pragmatic, the other mystical, the pair sets out on a
collision course, each unaware of the other's existence.
Threatened by his own notoriety, the white man assumes
the name James Otis. Vowing not to display grief to his
fellow warriors under his true name, the red man calls him
Worm after his father. Like Doroteo Arango/Pancho Villa,
they thus enter each other's sphere of combat outfitted in
borrowed armor. The machinery in motion, an amused Fate
settles back to watch.

As the hunters follow the spoor of rumors and chance
sightings to the lair of the white buffalo, Sales makes no
attempt to conceal his debt to Herman Melville other than
to go him one better and deliver two Ahabs for the price of
one. They do not seek merely a dumb brute any more than
did *Moby Dick*'s fixated mariner, but an amorphous Evil as
old as life and wearing a white mask. But this dragon is as
real as the Virginian's Trampas, not the windmill beloved
of Villa's revered Don Quixote, and the two warriors, sworn
enemies would each but learn his companion's true identity,
find themselves at last in the snowfield of their nightmares,
confronted weaponless by their red-eyed demon:

> . . . the vengeful humpback looked mammoth as it bore
> down to stomp him. Moonlight, garish after the dreary over-
> cast, danced like St. Elmo's fire across the scarlet horns. The
> night sky became cluttered with snow as the galloping split-
> hoofs kicked clouts into the air. . . . How anything that huge
> could move so fast was astonishing. The gap closed in two
> blinks of his startled eyes.

Perhaps predictably, but in the accepted manner of hero
tales, both men share equally in laying the monster to rest,
and Sales closes his uniquely fabulistic account of magical

and worldly values in a receding West with Wild Bill Hickok and Chief Crazy Horse riding their separate ways toward personal armageddon at Deadwood and the Little Big Horn.

10.

Only the Rocks Live Forever

The Assassination of Jesse James by the Coward Robert Ford (1984)

When does a writer's research and his use of it transcend drama and trespass upon reality? Sometimes, as is the case with Ron Hansen's *The Assassination of Jesse James by the Coward Robert Ford*, the only indication that the work is indeed fiction is its title.

Sir Walter Scott is generally credited with the invention of the historical novel by casting his own protagonists into the maelstrom of recorded events, a la *Ivanhoe*. For one hundred and fifty years this remained the norm, of which Will Henry and Thomas Berger took full advantage in *No Survivors* and *Little Big Man*, and which Douglas C. Jones continues to employ in his losers'-eye-view of the winning of the West. However, in recent years, emboldened by the example of the so-called new journalism as practiced by Tom Wolfe, Gay Talese, and Truman Capote, a number of writers have jettisoned this fictional baggage and dared to wander inside the thoughts and emotions of actual historical figures. Luminaries from Aaron Burr to Humphrey Bogart have come in for this treatment, with the result that many booksellers are undecided whether to shelve Gore Vidal's *Lincoln* under Fiction or Biography. The difference has to do with something as intangible and difficult to define as the author's own attitude, which has come to replace that of Scott's banished mythical heroes.

The florid editorialization in Hansen's title is tongue-in-cheek, an affectionate tribute to more innocent times when Frank Triplett's *The Life, Times, and Treacherous Death of Jesse James* could be regarded as serious biography. At that point, he abandons all dime-novel pretensions and adopts the same rich painterly style he used in *Desperadoes,* about the Dalton gang, to chronicle the squalid last days of the American Robin Hood who invented daylight bank robbery and became the country's first folk hero since Ethan Allen.

The story's central conflict is established early on, as Jesse and Frank James scrape together a sorry substitute for the old James-Younger coalition for one last raid at Blue Cut, Missouri. Included are young Dick Ford and his kid brother Bob, an awkward and callow youngster whose near-psychotic Jesse-worship yields a shoe box containing cigar-stubs smoked by the bandit and Bob's own tiresome rosary of the startling similarities between himself and his hero. Bob is perceived as Jesse's Fetch, a warped alter-ego feeding off the original's life force until he consumes him. Inquires Jesse: "I can't figure it out: do you want to be *like* me, or do you want to *be* me?"

Slowly and at times tediously—the effect of Hansen's blissful unconcern with pace can be like waiting for a fabulously well-crafted clock to tick—the narrative traces the gang's deterioration as mounting rewards for Jesse's capture dead or alive erode his trust in the men around him and they in turn plot against him in their own defense. Convinced that a partner is informing on him, he marches the man into the woods and executes him. The Fords, informers themselves, kill a James cousin to prevent exposure. Meanwhile the sham of friendship continues, with Jesse and Bob mouthing country platitudes and circling each other like wolves seeking an opening. The tension is macabre.

In his zeal to capture the texture of a time, Hansen draws heavily from contemporary newspapers, sometimes with results as gray as the columns in which they were printed. The corollary between the assassination of President Garfield and Ford's slowly awakening determination to do in Jesse James is hammered home a little too soundly. The shot that will end this relentless underscoring is welcomed in relief.

The story doesn't end there, however, and in a lengthy epilogue, Bob Ford is shown living out his remaining years under the cloud of his reputation as "the dirty little coward that shot Mr. Howard." This telescoped section is in some ways the best in a book that moves as slowly and carefully as some of its characters speak.

Slog though he may, Hansen is a master of language and a deadly manipulator of the rogue verb. Horses "clout" through snowdrifts; gunsmoke "balloons" from the brown muzzles of rifles and six-shooters. Some passages are suitable for framing:

> So they remained in the woodrows and neither talked nor smoked nor stamped their boots to the earth. Cold watered their eyes and cemented their mittens to their rifle stocks and turned their feet into flatirons. . . .

Assassination blends an artist's eye with a hands-on knowledge of the West to produce a study in gray, brown, and scarlet of the tawdry reality behind romantic folklore. Often staid, sometimes forced, it is throughout an accurate portrayal of men at odds with their own myths.

Centennial (1974)

> When the earth was already ancient, of an age incomprehensible to man, an event of basic importance occurred in the area which would later be known as Colorado.

The style of this passage from James Michener's *Centennial* is as singular as a thumbprint. "My first reports may go a little deeper than you intended," the fictional author of this book-within-a-book warns his publishers—and we are instantly transported back to that primordial era when the bedrock upon which the city of Centennial would be founded was shoved into place by a volcanic upheaval.

This approach, unique among westerns, is typical of the writer who turned the conquest of Hawaii and the history of South Africa into epics and their titles into household words. It is diametrically opposed to the attitude of Thomas Berger and Brian Garfield, taking its facts straight and without frills, but is to some extent a return to Scott in that all of its characters, notwithstanding brief incursions by such as Daniel Boone, Chester Alan Arthur, and Lewis and Clark, are imaginary, although if one reads closely enough he will recognize the occasional Nat Love and George Armstrong Custer thinly disguised. Like a marine biologist reconstructing the life in a pond from a drop of water under his microscope, Michener recasts the western experience as it relates to a city of his invention.

Bypassing the prehistoric conceit and the lives and deaths of brontosauri and giant beavers as fascinating but unnecessary padding, we find that *Centennial* really begins more than a hundred pages in with the appearance of the Arapaho hero Lame Beaver. It gains momentum when the French-Canadian trader Pasquinel paddles into view, enters Guthrie country when he strikes a partnership with Alexander McKeag, an expatriate Scot in search of personal freedom, and latches onto more familiar western territory, that of Wister and Grey and Schaefer and eventually Swarthout, with the entrance of Levi Zendt, the Mennonite settler who brings a measure of civilization to the region and opens the gate for "potato king" Hans Brumbaugh, who chains the South Platte; John Skimmerhorn, who brings cattle to it in the wake of his demented father's massacre of Lame Beaver's progeny; and the Wendells, whose theater-bred perfidy greases the skids for all the corruptors, swindlers, and victims to follow.

Michener's objective method offers a spare but heartrending glimpse of changes in progress:

> Two long weeks they spent in the saddle, chasing illusions and finding emptiness. They grew so weak from lack of food, they could scarcely ride, but still they searched, and in the end they might have perished, actually starved to death on their prairie, had they not stumbled upon an area north of the Arkansas where the carcasses of eighty-nine buffalo lay rotting in the sun.
>
> The men were so famished that one actually ate some decayed meat, but Red Wolf saw the folly of this and spurred his horse so that he stood between his men and the meat. Holding his right hand aloft, he gradually drove them back, and after a while the one who had eaten was gripped in dreadful pain, dying with foam on his lips, and the others acknowledged the wisdom of their chief.

"Only the rocks live forever," proclaimed Lame Beaver, fifty years before this event.

Because of his prolificity and phenomenal popularity, Michener is sometimes branded a hack by critics ignorant of the writing process and envious of the metabolism that enables him to crank out weighty tomes on a regular basis. His research is impeccable and his stark style is unrelenting. He has moreover a Tolstoyan talent for manipulating a large ensemble cast without confusing his readers over who is doing what to whom, a basic and often overlooked quality in good fiction. He writes with a deceptive simplicity that defies dating and renders the past immediate.

Centennial invites no comparison to any other western title, although most of its characters and incidents have his-

torical parallels. Michener, a master of the epic, alone assumes
the task of spreading before his readers the complete saga of
the frontier from its wild origins to the troubled present.
Certainly anyone else who attempted to go back as far would
be accused of imitation. Like the West itself, the book grows
narrower with each chapter, crowding the broad land where
giants walked with lesser characters, meaner situations. Its
hero is the land, and like the best heroes it is not the same
when we leave it as when we made its acquaintance. As much
can be said of its literature. *The Virginian* and *Centennial* are
about the same things, but they are not similar. If they were,
there would be little reason to read beyond Owen Wister.

Postscript
Into a New Century?

"Almost every American of whatever age, sex and station in life likes a good western and always has."

The words, penned in 1953 by Luke Short in his foreword to *Bad Men and Good,* the first Western Writers of America anthology, ring with sad irony in the 1980s, amid redundantly dire predictions of the western's imminent demise and observations that the current climate of social and political unrest at home and splinter wars in Asia and the Middle East will not tolerate stories about the struggle for a forgotten frontier. The feminist hysteria and activism among the pampered descendants of the racial and ethnic martyrs from whose graves sprang the thorny weed of civilization have called into question the very values expressed by the form, so that even the heroic image of Gary Cooper walking alone down the dusty main thoroughfare of the "High Noon" set is somehow considered shameful. Thus the siege of civilization continues.

Part of the blame must fall upon that majority of western writers whose distaste for research drove them to construct their own mythology, complete with a cast and creed that they could build on without need for consultation, secure in the knowledge that those things they invented could only be measured against their own painted backdrop. In their portable tabletop West, the eighteen-month life of the Pony Express spans years, and Doc Holliday, twenty-nine years old at the time of the O.K. Corral shootout, shuffles into that arena a tubercular old man. The James-Younger gang, which rode or shot down a little girl while quitting Liberty, Kansas, after the raid on the bank, are sad rebel heroes in fresh linen, and Pat Garrett, who gunned down Billy the Kid from ambush in New Mexico, faces the young desperado in open combat under the noon sun.

It stands to reason that beneath the constant bombardment of these straight-faced falsehoods, an increasingly sophisticated public would turn away, if not toward something more plausible, then toward a different form with a fresh mythology. This explains the proliferation on television and in the movies and on bookstore racks of cops and robbers swapping lead in an urban frontier, and of spacemen attired in neo-Renaissance doublets and helmets doing battle in the plains of the stratosphere with aliens who speak with upper-class British accents. Lies, after all, are not unacceptable; merely those twice told.

Nor are they confined to the various frontiers, as witness late depictions of the New South as a sunny place where good old boys and redneck sheriffs chase one another in juiced-up cars over endless dirt roads, and of the 1960s as an era when those unwashed drop-out hedonists the hippies preached and practiced universal love and cared about the state of the world. But none of these Never-Never Lands is as lovingly and elaborately detailed as the one that the literary rabble has substituted for the Old West, and a society with a new interest in its historical and genetic heritage soon loses its fascination with colored beads.

This reverse was a long time coming. Decades before "The Great Train Robbery," eastern readers, awakened to the adventure of the West by Custer's serialized memoirs and by fanciful accounts of the explorations of Meriwether Lewis and William Clark, devoured the once-removed dime thrillers by the tens of millions. *The Virginian* and *Riders of the Purple Sage,* which appeared even as the frontier was still playing out its last chapter, outsold every other book published between the turn of the century and World War I. Motion pictures brought these indelible images to fluttering life, and Cecil B. DeMille's "The Squawman" and the aforementioned "Great Train Robbery" did more than any other feature to transfer Edison's toy from tin crank-boxes in the backs of Brooklyn candy stores to the grand Art Deco palaces where William S. Hart and Tom Mix made faces under ten-gallon Stetsons and, later, an incredibly youthful John Wayne stepped out of the Monument Valley desert into the sweep and clatter of John Ford's magnificent "Stagecoach" in the era of sound.

In print, the western had made the natural progression from dime novels to the pulps, so called because of the coarse paper glued between garish covers on which demonic Indians constantly terrorized buxom women in gingham shirts three sizes too small and tight jeans anticipating the Jordache Look by four decades. Although the pulp phenomenon would be remembered for the creation of the "hard-boiled" American detective story, the western remained as much a staple in *Black Mask* and *Spicy Stories* as it was in *Frontier Stories* and *Northwest Romances* until the World War II paper shortage and the rise of the comic book killed off the pulps.

Television discovered the western early on, with such diverse entries as "The Lone Ranger" and "Gunsmoke" making the jump from radio to a home screen already filled with Wyatt Earps and Bat Mastersons and Yancy Derringers and Hopalong Cassidys and Sugarfeet. Gene Autry and Roy Rogers set Tom Mix to music, "Sky King" sent Shane aloft, and

Walt Disney put every other child in the United States into buckskins and Davy Crockett coonskin caps.

In a multi-million-dollar move to win back the audience it had lost to television, the motion picture industry unveiled a wide-screen gimmick developed by French director Abel Gance in 1927, renamed it Cinemascope, and selected the western for its vast spaces and breathtaking mountainscapes as its star. It flourished under this flattering attention even as Cinemascope withered and died for lack of artistic intimacy and theaters capable of screening the attenuated rectangular features. Today the wide-screen western alone remains fresh and free of the elephantine overstatement of the Ben Hurs, Cleopatras, and other spectaculars of the era. The form even managed to survive 3-D.

Meanwhile the reading audience was building, and Luke Short, long before his death elevated rival Louis L'Amour to the throne of King of Western Novels by forfeit, found his way into as many private libraries as Zane Grey had twenty years before him. By 1953, with the noise of hoofbeats and gunfire emanating from ten million television sets and the music of the Sons of the Pioneers warbling from as many phonographs, Short could attribute the lion's share of the annual paperback revenue of $63,000,000 to westerns.

It was by no means an entirely domestic phenomenon. In France, West Germany, the Soviet Union, and a rapidly westernizing postwar Japan, cowboy movies thirty years old and the translated works of western writers dead and forgotten in their own country ran up figures unknown since Ned Buntline. (Years before the war, young Adolf Hitler found a role model in Shatterhand, the Indian antagonist in German writer Karl May's novels of the West.)

Whether Vietnam changed all that, or whether it came along just as the change was starting, is the stuff of another debate. Certainly, daily televised combat footage on the Six O'Clock News did little to romanticize another war against native guerrillas a hundred years earlier, and with Indian activists occupying Alcatraz and Wounded Knee, there seemed little cause for pride in the conquest of the prairie. A man on horseback appeared impossibly archaic when Soviet tanks were trundling into Czechoslovakia, the six-shooter on his hip hardly heroic after the firearm assassinations of two Kennedys, a King, and four faceless students at Kent State. Why read of Jesse James when youngsters in army surplus were hurling bricks and antipersonnel bombs through the windows of military recruitment offices on behalf of world peace?

Italy and Spain, which like most of Europe continued to revere things American while scorning Americans themselves, introduced sorely needed authenticity into the western film. In their features, overlooked American actors roamed celluloid Continental plains looking for profit, not honor, carrying period weapons in place of the streamlined, nickel-plated, stag-handled Peacemakers that had won Hollywood's West. Although these "spaghetti westerns" are often blamed for killing off the form, they instead managed to keep it alive during a dry time by offering a surface realism unseen on film since "Cripple Creek Barroom" in the days of the nickelodeon. Disillusioned viewers stood in line to see these surreal tamperings with a sacred formula. And a scant five years before critic Pauline Kael announced the death of the movie western, Paul Newman and Robert Redford took advantage of a frontier newly reopened by the Europeans to sing a song of youthful rebellion a la "Bonnie and Clyde" in "Butch Cassidy and the Sundance Kid," sparking a brief, brilliant flare-up of iconoclastic oaters in theaters and on television.

Brief it was. By the early 1970s, only three western television series were left on the air, all of them geriatric. "The Virginian" closed out its run under an inexplicable new title, followed closely by "Bonanza" after fifteen years, the last five without a sense of humor and the last season without one of its most popular stars and minus its distinctive musical theme. Then, after an unprecedented twenty years on top of a long radio run, "Gunsmoke" ended, leaving the medium without a weekly western for the first time since the late 1940s. In their place blossomed a plethora of "relevant" social dramas about idealistic high school teachers and upwardly mobile urban minority types, none of which survived the decade.

Western writing had suffered for longer, as had the entire book industry under the onslaught of television, the exercise fad, and electronic video games. Most of the westerns being published were reprints and new works by writers left over from the pulp era who had lost touch with an audience born after World War II. Their heroes seemed to personify a hated Establishment and their concern for law and order might have come from the oratory of politicians whose rallies and conventions the youths were demonstrating against. Traditionally, when in doubt, art turns to spectacle and sex, and this time the western veered in the latter direction. The Adult Western was born.

The late Playboy Press generally receives the credit or the blame for having given birth to this hybrid, but a small paperback publisher in California, Major Books (also defunct), anticipated Playboy with a line of violent and sexually explicit westerns in the mid-1970s whose titles, among them *Buzzard Bait* and *Slaughter at Crucifix Canyon*, are self-explanatory. Jove introduced the factory approach inspired by Pinnacle Books' enormously successful "Executioner" crime series, issuing new "Longarm" titles monthly under an umbrella pseudonym for a gang of veteran western writers left marketless by changing tastes. Zebra and Ace Charter fell into line with "Gunn" and "The Gunsmith"; and soon the stores were filled with uniform covers and enough sex—in beds, bathtubs, on Indian blankets and horseback, in wigwams in Wyoming and under the big, bright stars of

Texas—to turn the Rockies blue. Sometimes slickly written but more often hacked out in two or three weeks of one-armed afternoons, the stories are usually bloody and por-nographic retellings of themes standardized as far back as Buntline and Prentiss Ingraham, and have been the subject of considerable shrill denunciation on the part of reactionaries in the western field. But for all the hyperbole about the danger they pose to the future of the western, their extreme popularity has provided a lucrative learning ground for new writers deprived of the pulp school, rescued a number of veteran writers from the welfare rolls, and kept warm the western racks in bookstores lest science fiction and self-help freeze them out entirely.

The western is often reported to be in critical condition, dated and pointless in the world of Vietnam and Watergate (and, earlier, of the Great Depression and Auschwitz). These reports invariably precede dramatically renewed interest in the form. For no genre ever dies.

Western classics have without exception concerned them-selves with authenticity, but only recently has the entire genre begun to question the commonly accepted iconography. This evolution is salutary and will continue as writers and readers learn that the western need not snag itself on the monoto-nously towering heroes of Louis L'Amour ex-*Hondo* or the pompous psychological pretension of Van Tilburg Clark's multi-editioned *Ox-Bow Incident,* and discover that the Wister Trace, while long and winding, eventually leads back to its source.

As wide as *The Big Sky* and *Centennial,* as narrow as *The Shootist,* as romantic as *Shane,* as realistic as *The Assassi-nation of Jesse James,* as poetic as *Riders of the Purple Sage,* as satirical as *Little Big Man,* as philosophical as *The Vir-ginian,* as grim as *The Ox-Bow Incident* and *The Treasure of the Sierra Madre,* as much fun as *True Grit,* and about as many subjects as there are titles in its category, the frontier in fiction is America's major contribution to world literature. Allowing room for the idiosyncrasies of the occasional bookseller, frontier fiction will continue to produce classics, if only because that is what is expected of a national art form.

Bibliography

A

Anonymous. *The Dalton Brothers.* Chicago: Laird & Lee Publishers, 1892.

B

Bailey, Tom. *The Comanche Wars.* Derby, Conn.: Monarch Books, Inc., 1963.

Beckwourth, James P. *The Life and Adventures of James P. Beckwourth.* New York: Harper & Brothers, 1856.

Berger, Thomas. *Little Big Man.* New York: Dial Press, 1964.

Blevins, Winfred. *Give Your Heart to the Hawks.* New York: Nash Publishing Corporation, 1973.

Breihan, Carl W. *Great Gunfighters of the West.* Tenafly, N.J.: Naylor Company, 1962.

Brown, Dee. *Bury My Heart at Wounded Knee.* New York: Holt, Rinehart, and Winston, 1971.

C

Capps, Benjamin. *Sam Chance.* New York: Ace Books, 1965.

Cobb, Humphrey. *Paths of Glory.* New York: Viking Press, 1935.

Connell, Evan S. *Son of the Morning Star.* San Francisco: North Point Press, 1984.

Custer, George A. *My Life on the Plains.* New York: Sheldon & Co., 1874.

D

Dary, David. *Cowboy Culture.* New York: Alfred A. Knopf, Inc., 1981.

E

Everson, William K. *A Pictorial History of the Western Film.* Secaucus, N.J.: Citadel Press, Inc., 1969.

F

Fisher, Vardis. *Mountain Man.* New York: Pocket Books, 1967 (reprint).

G

Garfield, Brian. *Wild Times.* New York: Simon & Schuster, 1978.

Garrett, Pat F. *The Authentic Life of Billy the Kid, the Noted Desperado of the Southwest.* Santa Fe: New Mexican Printing & Publishing Co., 1882.

Gogol, Nikolai. *Taras Bulba.* Moscow: Foreign Languages Publishing House, no date (reprint).

Golding, William. *Lord of the Flies.* New York: G. P. Putnam's Sons, 1959.

Goodstone, Tony. *The Pulps.* New York: Chelsea House Publishers, 1970.

Graham, W. A. *The Custer Myth.* Harrisburg, Pa.: Telegraph Press, 1953.

Grey, Zane. *Riders of the Purple Sage.* New York: Harper & Brothers Publishers, Inc., 1912.

————. *The Thundering Herd.* New York: Harper & Brothers Publishers, Inc., 1925.

————. *The U.P. Trail.* New York: Harper & Brothers Publishers, Inc., 1918.

Grinnell, George Bird. *The Cheyenne Indians.* New Haven, Conn.: Yale University Press, 1923.

Guthrie, A. B., Jr. *The Big Sky.* Boston: Houghton Mifflin Co., 1952.

————. *The Way West.* Boston: Houghton Mifflin Co., 1949.

H

Hansen, Ron. *The Assassination of Jesse James by the Coward Robert Ford.* New York: Alfred A. Knopf, 1983.

————. *Desperadoes.* New York: Alfred A. Knopf, 1979.

Haven, Charles T., and Belden, Frank A. *A History of the Colt Revolver.* New York: Bonanza Books, 1978.

Henry, Will. *From Where the Sun Now Stands.* New York: Bantam Books, 1960.

————. *No Survivors.* New York: Random House, Inc., 1950.

Horn, Tom. *Life of Tom Horn.* Denver: Louthan Book Co., 1904.

Hotchkiss, Bill. *The Medicine Calf.* New York: W. W. Norton & Co., 1981.

Hyams, Jay. *The Life and Times of the Western Movie.* New York: W. H. Smith Publishers, Inc., 1983.

J

Jones, Douglas C. *Arrest Sitting Bull.* New York: Charles Scribner's Sons, 1977.
————. *The Court-Martial of George Armstrong Custer.* New York: Charles Scribner's Sons, 1976.
————. *A Creek Called Wounded Knee.* New York: Charles Scribner's Sons, 1978.
Joseph, Alan M., Jr., ed. *The American Heritage Book of Indians.* New York: American Heritage Publishing Co., Inc., 1961.

K

Kelton, Elmer. *The Day the Cowboys Quit.* Garden City: Doubleday & Co., Inc., 1971.
Kupfer, Allen C., and Sheehan, David L. III. *The West: A Trivia Quiz Book.* New York: Warner Books, 1985.

L

L'Amour, Louis. *Comstock Lode.* New York: Bantam Books, 1981.
————. *Hondo.* Greenwich, Conn.: Fawcett Publications, Inc., 1953.
Le May, Alan. *The Searchers.* New York: Ace Books, 1980 (reprint).
Leonard, Elmore. *Hombre.* New York: Ballantine Books, 1961.

M

Melville, Herman. *Moby Dick.* Secaucus, N.J.: Longriver Press, 1976 (reprint).

Metz, Leon Claire. *The Shooters.* El Paso: Mangan Books, 1976.

Michener, James. *Centennial.* New York: Random House, Inc., 1974.

Myatt, F. *The Illustrated Encyclopedia of 19th Century Firearms.* London: Salamander Books, Ltd., 1979.

N

The National Encyclopedia. New York: P. F. Collier & Son, 1932.

Newark, Peter. *The Illustrated Encyclopedia of the Old West.* New York: Gallery Books, 1980.

Nordyke, Lewis. *John Wesley Hardin: Texas Gunman.* New York: William Morrow & Co., 1957.

P

Parkman, Francis. *The Oregon Trail.* New York: *Knickerbocker Magazine,* 1847.

Portis, Charles. *True Grit.* New York: Simon & Schuster, 1968.

R

Richards, Norman V. *Cowboy Movies.* New York: Gallery Books, 1984.

Richter, Conrad. *The Sea of Grass.* New York: Curtis Publishing Co., 1936.

S

Sales, Richard. *The White Buffalo.* New York: Simon & Schuster, 1975.

Sandoz, Mari. *The Battle of the Little Big Horn.* Philadelphia: J. B. Lippincott, 1966.

Schaefer, Jack. *Monte Walsh.* Boston: Houghton Mifflin Co., 1963.

——. *Shane.* Boston: Houghton Mifflin Co., 1949.

Seidman, Lawrence Ivan. *Once in the Saddle.* New York: Alfred A. Knopf, 1973.

Sell, Henry Blackman, and Weybright, Victor. *Buffalo Bill and the Wild West.* New York: New American Library, 1959 (reprint).

Settle, William A., Jr. *Jesse James Was His Name.* Columbia: University of Missouri Press, 1966.

Shirley, Glenn. *Law West of Fort Smith.* Lincoln: University of Nebraska Press, 1968.

Shirreffs, Gordon D. *The Untamed Breed.* New York: Fawcett Gold Medal Books, 1981.

Shorris, Earl. *Under the Fifth Sun.* New York: Delacorte Press, 1980.

Shulman, Arthur, and Youman, Roger. *The Television Years.* New York: Popular Library, 1973.

Swarthout, Glendon. *The Shootist.* Garden City: Doubleday & Co., Inc., 1975.

T

Time-Life Editors. *The Old West.* New York: Time-Life Books, 1974-1979.

Traven, B. *The Treasure of the Sierra Madre.* New York: Alfred A. Knopf, 1935.

Triplett, Frank. *The Life, Times, and Treacherous Death of Jesse James.* St. Louis: J. H. Chambers & Co., 1882.

Tuska, Jon. *The Filming of the West.* Garden City: Doubleday & Co., Inc., 1976.

V

Van Tilburg Clark, Walter. *The Ox-Bow Incident.* New York: Random House, Inc., 1940.

Vestal, Stanley. *Queen of Cowtowns: Dodge City.* New York: Harper & Row Publishers, 1952.

W

Walker, Dale, ed. *Will Henry's West.* El Paso: Texas Western Press, 1984.

Western Writers of America. *Bad Men and Good.* New York: Dodd, Mead & Co., Inc., 1953.

Wister, Owen. *The Virginian.* New York: Airmont Publishing Co., 1964 (reprint).

Wyatt, Will. *The Secret of the Sierra Madre.* Garden City: Doubleday & Co., Inc., 1980.

Y

Yost, Nellie Snyder. *Buffalo Bill.* Chicago: Swallow Press, 1979.